Foul is Fair

Book One of the Fair Folk Chronicles
by Jeffrey Cook and Katherine Perkins

Fair winds and following seas.

Jeffrey Cook

Dedicated to the late Sir Terry Pratchett, whose blend of nonsense and indignant good sense resonated both with a teenage girl whose e-mail he answered and with a guy who appreciated a good Blues Brothers joke. He certainly warned us that no one said elves were nice.

Table of Contents

Chapter 1: Attention

Lani may have been saying something about "a matter of life and death," but Megan couldn't hear her for sure over her medical timer. Four o'clock meant the orange pills, 40 mg total. The multicolored ones in the other bottle were for the morning. She took 80 mg of those with breakfast. That was a different timer, of course.

"Really?" Lani asked. "You're going to take that right now?"

"Need to." Megan downed them with a whole glass of water, as directed.

"You need medication, yeah. You were already on medication before. Then she kept switching doctors until one would... you were doing better! Your grades were already going up on the old dose. Remember?"

Megan supposed she did remember. 40 mg of the multicolored pills in the morning, 40 in the afternoon. Lani would generally remind her during the first break in their afternoon study sessions. The second break had been for art projects and stuff. Yeah, that had happened. The grades had gone up a little.

"It still was hard. Still had symptoms," Megan said as she picked up a composition book with just one streak of orange marker across the cover.

"It's going to be hard. That's a thing that happens! And doodling is not a sym—" Lani sighed. "I'm sorry. Can we talk?"

"Can't we just get on the phone tonight?"

"When your Mom's home?"

"She doesn't mind a phone call as long as I'm in bed on time. So we can talk then like usual." Megan put pencil to paper. '$[(x-h)^2/a^2] - [(y-k)^2/b^2] = 1$'

"'Usual' has gotten really relative lately, Megan. And this is urgent, and ..." Did Lani normally stop in the middle of sentences like that? Megan couldn't remember. '$[(x-h)^2/a^2] - [(y-k)^2/b^2] = 1$,' she wrote.

"There's some things you just aren't supposed to hear first over the phone," Lani said.

"I've got a lot to do," Megan said. $'[(x-h)^2/a^2]-[(y-k)^2/b^2]=1'$ "That conic sections stuff for math." Math had never been Megan's strongest subject. She'd always understood the basic concepts, at least once they were repeated for her, but little mistakes crept early into her calculation and threw everything off. Best way to fix it, she now figured, was repetition. $'[(x-h)^2/a^2]-[(y-k)^2/b^2]=1'$

The upcoming conic sections project was a big deal. She might get her first A+ outside art or music classes in a long time, if she stuck to the plan and didn't blow it. Not that she'd gotten any + in art class this semester, what with whatever problem Mrs. Chang had these days that made her keep asking Megan if something was wrong, but that was beside the point.

Lani was still trying to talk. "But—" but Megan was already getting to work. $'[(x-h)^2/a^2]-[(y-k)^2/b^2]=1'$

* * *

Lani stood there for a moment, in a room silent except for pencil scratches. She looked at the bookshelf. She looked at the bottle of multicolored pills. She looked at the neat little row of composition books, all of their covers drenched in various colors of marker. Lani knew the margins of every page were filled with drawings of trees and butterflies, rough doodles and intricate patterns. Even Megan's posters followed the theme, hand-drawn landscapes and blown-up photographs decorated every wall. None of them were new. All of them were made before Ms. O'Reilly had found a doctor willing to 'finally fix it properly.'

Lani also knew that the composition book Megan was working in now had doodles only on the first two pages. Then the pencils marks were solely class notes, and the markers were only for highlighting.

Lani looked at the bottle of orange pills. She looked at Megan, whose right hand occasionally rose to brush the long auburn curls out of her face while she worked. Megan copied the same set of equations over and over and over again with her left hand, trying to commit them to memory through sheer mechanical tenacity.

Lani looked at the clock. There was still plenty of time before Ms. O'Reilly came home. There was technically plenty of time to tell Megan what she needed to know. Part of Lani felt sure that if this emergency had arisen sophomore year, they'd already have a plan right now. Granted, it would possibly have been three half-plans and two intricately illustrated visual aids, but it would have been better than standing here knowing nothing important she said would be heard or recognized.

Lani left the room. She left the off-white little house on 47th. Her own place wasn't a long walk, though the steep hills of West Seattle made for good exercise and the early evening air helped to clear her head. She checked in with her mother and made sure her little brother was too occupied with his LEGOs to come spy on her, though she intended to listen for any calls of 'Makani Noa Kahale, get back in here this instant,' just in case. Then she headed into the backyard. She spent the last minutes of proper daylight walking around the multi-tiered garden, passing through the pair of wooden trellises and archways that decorated the carefully laid-out path, before settling into the gazebo in the middle of the rock garden, next to the small decorative fish pond. The limited lots of the neighborhood didn't leave a lot of room, but, true to her family's usual style, every inch was filled with something, and somehow, they'd made it all fit.

No strangers were likely to peek into the backyard. If they did, they wouldn't be likely to look into the gazebo, as they'd be busy wondering why such fancy garden structures were built for a bunch of pumpkins grown with more enthusiasm than skill. If anyone had looked, however, they might have seen the short, stocky sixteen-year-old sitting on a bench and staring as a crow flitted down from above and landed on the railing of the gazebo. The bird looked at her quizzically, while Lani paid more attention to the butterfly perched on the crow's head.

"We're out of options. If we're going to tell her, she's going to have to listen. Do it tonight. The orange ones, right side of the bookshelf."

The wind rustled through the trees.

"Just the orange ones. I'm not going to get in the way of her being a functional human being."

Lani looked at the crow as it started to take off again. "You know what I mean," she answered what no stranger would have heard.

Chapter 2: Transitions

Megan woke to her mother's voice. "Why is the window open?" Megan unburied her head from under her pillow, squinting at the light filtering in as the curtains waved erratically.

"Don't know," she admitted.

"Well, try to be more careful. The rain getting in would be a problem. Rise and shine. It's the bus today. I can't give you a ride because of event meetings with three potential clients. Let's go. We've had a good schedule going for weeks, so let's keep at it."

When her mother left the room, Megan finished working herself out of bed, moving to the mirror and untangling her mop of reddish curls. She normally wouldn't wish her mother's hair, long since trained to her severe buns, on anyone, but some days, it'd certainly make brushing easier. As soon as she had her hair tied back, she checked her pills. Five minutes left on the timer meant five minutes to get to breakfast. Megan figured it was a good thing she'd finally adopted her mother's habit of laying her clothes out the night before, like she was supposed to.

The timer went off just as she got to the kitchen table. There was no getting out of eating. Megan poured her cereal, added milk, picked up the spoon, and took a breath. Bite by bite, she shoveled it into her mouth, chewed, and swallowed. Breakfast was the most important meal of the day. For one thing, the multi-colored pills functioned better with food. She wouldn't need a timer at lunch, at least. There was the school bell to remind her to eat then.

Megan made the bus stop just in time. Lani was already aboard from her earlier stop. She got up to let Megan have the window seat, as always. Megan took it with a "thanks," then stared ahead for a moment before remembering to get out her composition book.

"So...how is...everything?" Lani asked.

"Okay. I want to work on the next type of conic-section graph for math." The new formula was '$[(x-h)^2/a^2] + [(y-k)^2/b^2]=1.$'

Megan would need to keep straight which shape was which. She'd been thrown off so many times before. She started writing.

"Okay, that's...okay. Need any...help?"

"No, thanks."

School happened. Megan took notes. Her latest art assignment had not done well, and Mrs. Chang looked sad handing it back. Megan didn't know why. Her butterfly pictures had always gotten good grades before. For this one, she'd drawn a dozen identical butterflies, in even rows of four. Megan had no idea what Mrs. Chang's problem was.

Lani's remarks as Megan raised and lifted the fork through lunch seemed awkward. So did their conversation on the bus that afternoon. Was that Lani's Guilty Face? It was hard for Megan to tell anything with Lani anymore, but there'd be time to figure it out later. '$[(x-h)^2/a^2] + [(y-k)^2/b^2]=1.$'

Lani didn't get off at Megan's stop this time. Megan let herself into the little off-white house and poured herself a glass of water. She tried to work on the formula. '$[(x-h)^2/a^2] + [(y-k)^2/b^2]=1.$'

The timer went off. She took the orange pills with her glass of water. Something tasted strange, but Megan tried to get back to work. She got out the graph paper with the coordinate system, plotted out the horizontal curves, and properly labeled it with the appropriate equation, double checking three times. Then it was time for the vertical oval. In the course of drawing it, Megan became aware of the fact that she had a headache.

She got up to get herself another glass of water. Having drunk it, she was putting the glass away, intending to get back to her desk, when her stomach growled. It almost took Megan a moment to remember what to do about something like that. It wasn't even suppertime, and she was hungry.

Half an hour later, Megan was on the couch with her third banana in one hand and a 2001 photo album in the other. She looked at the last photograph pasted into it, above careful calligraphy that read "*Sheila, Ric, and Megan.*"

Sheila O'Reilly looked tired, certainly, but there was still something in that tired smile that Megan never tended to see in her mother.

Megan was newly two, her face covered in ice cream. Holding her was a lithe-looking man with long hair, and somehow she always knew he had a voice like chocolate: dark, deep, and rich. Megan had always told herself that she was silly, that she'd been too young to properly remember now what his voice sounded like. But she knew it all the same.

Her mother's car pulled into the driveway. Megan put the photo album back on its shelf and hurried back to her desk. What had she been doing? Right, she'd been labeling the graph. Somewhere.

In the morning, which seemed to come so much sooner, with much less counting sheep than usual the night before, the headache was worse. It was a good thing her mother could drive her, because Megan was just slightly behind schedule. During the drive, her mother occasionally glanced anxiously at her, asking after the headache, which Megan had not been able to hide. Megan shrugged it off. She looked at the charcoal pantsuit and pinned up hair, thinking of the green jacket and long flowing hair in the photograph. She looked at the anxious expression and thought of the smile. She didn't say anything, though. Some things they'd long since learned not to talk about.

School happened again, fortunately on a Friday. They were reminded that their assignment on graphing conic sections was due Monday. At lunch, Megan bit into her sandwich and almost, for a moment, savored the peanut butter goodness before clutching her head a little. Lani really did look worried. She looked worried on the bus ride home, too, whenever Megan looked up from the circle equations, which were '$(x-h)^2+(y-k)^2=r^2$.' But Megan almost thought that part of Lani's worried expression looked almost... hopeful?

She got home, let herself in, got out the graph paper, and went for the water. When the timer went off, she took her pills. The taste was strange again—citrus, she decided—but maybe it was something to do with the headache.

She checked over the listed equations. She drew a small circle to the left of the leftmost horizontal curve and carefully labeled its equation. Then she drew another on the right of the rightmost curve. Then an additional pair on each side. And two diagonal line segments, jutting out from the top of the oval. Megan had to eventually stop herself, go back, and check all the equations for each component before writing them. Then she sat for a moment, looked at the spotted butterfly on the carefully labeled graph paper, and got out her colored pencils.

Chapter 3: Painted Lady

After supper came chores, starting with the dishes. Then her mother retired to the living room to read the paper while Megan wandered out to get the mail.

She supposed, at first, that it was her headache, but the world seemed brighter or more vibrant than usual as she made her way out of the house. Halfway to the mailbox, she found her eyes drawn to the Halloween decorations displayed up and down the block. Some were just lonely little cutouts taped to the insides of windows or the outsides of doors. More than a few houses had pumpkins, carved with varying degrees of artistic talent, laid out on their porches. A couple of the houses had gone overboard with orange lights or lawn ornaments.

She didn't focus on any one setup, instead finding her mind wandering and trying to place when all of these had gone up. That train of thought led to her noting her own house, the sole one not decorated in the least for the holiday. She still had a few of her own decorations from past years, but it struck her as wrong, somehow, to just put them up without doing something new. Nothing was occurring to her, and, of course, she had some homework left. Maybe she could make something once she'd finished and checked the equations, though. She was having trouble remembering them.

She wasn't sure quite how long she spent outside in the fading light of dusk, looking around at the displays or lack of display. Shaking off the trail of thoughts, and hoping her mother hadn't missed her yet, if she'd been too long, she made the rest of the trip to the mailbox.

Sitting on the mailbox, canting its head at her quizzically, was a crow. They were common enough in the neighborhood, but none of them had ever let her approach quite so close before without flying off. This one, however, showed no signs of moving. As she took another step forward, a splash of color on the crow's back became more evident.

Megan blinked a couple of times, sure she was seeing things. Despite the efforts to clear her head, she became certain that, yes, in fact, resting on the back of the crow's neck was a butterfly. Its wings were black, white, and orange, but had somehow been ripped at the edges to more jaggedly reveal the pink-and-brown underside.

As she was simultaneously trying to remember the type of butterfly and thinking how sad it was that something had happened to its wings, she came around to the thought that she shouldn't be seeing what she was seeing. As that thought hit her, she also noted that the crow was looking at her like she was the strange one. A bird was silently evaluating her while wearing a — Painted Lady! That was it. She knew them. They were so common throughout the world that they were also called Cosmopolitan butterflies. Despite that, they didn't get up to Seattle very often, though she'd seen a few before.

"You need to talk to Lani."

Megan blinked and looked around. She heard the wind whispering through the trees, which was odd, because the branches weren't blowing.

"Over here. And you need to talk to Lani."

Another glance around, and Megan shifted her attention back towards the crow. As she did, the light started to dim as the sun slipped below the horizon.

"You need to talk to Lani," repeated the little wisp of a woman, sitting astride the crow's neck. She was delicate, even for her tiny size, and her skin was amber-colored. She wore a light dress, black with odd white zebra striping. The tattered orange-patterned wings were still there, though.

"What happened to your wings?" Megan heard herself asking, out of all of the questions that were fighting the headache to rise to the fore in her brain.

"I'll tell you the story later," the tiny girl promised. "But I only have a few more seconds before you won't be able to hear me." A pause. "Yet. We'll talk a lot more later. Right now, you need to promise me that you'll talk to Lani."

The crow cawed, and the tiny girl patted it on the head. "Yes, Count. You're right. Megan, you need to promise to meet with Lani, somewhere private. And you need to listen, really listen, when she talks."

"His name is Count?" Megan managed. It made more sense, at the moment, to ask than anything else occurring to her.

"Yes, yes. I'll tell you that story too. And where babies come from. And where faeries come from. And why you can't tickle yourself. Later. Promise me."

"Okay," Megan managed. She stared a few moments longer, as if expecting the crow or the butterfly to either disappear or make sense. "I promise," she added.

The pair glanced at each other in satisfaction. A few moments later, the scene changed again. It was only slightly less surreal, seeing a butterfly on a crow's back again. Megan blinked once more, trying to form another coherent question. Before she could manage, the crow lifted off, bearing the butterfly away again.

Megan continued trying to frame questions, even after they were gone. She walked around a little more, staring around to make sure nothing else in the neighborhood had changed. She glanced back at her plain, undecorated off-white house and resolved, homework or no, to do something to decorate it this year. Probably after she talked to Lani.

Megan returned to the house, made sure her mother was occupied, and then headed to her room to call Lani. The phone picked up on the first ring. "Hello, Megan?"

"Yes. Someone says I need to talk to you. You won't believe me if I tell you who. I'm not sure I believe me."

"I bet I will. There was a crow involved, right?"

Chapter 4: Bad

Talking about it on the phone when Megan's mother was home hadn't been an option for Lani. Letting Megan walk to Lani's in the dark hadn't been an option for Megan's mother. Neither had driving her, or letting her ask Mrs. Kahale for an unscheduled ride. Megan really wished that Lani and her dad would finish putting Lani's car together already. Assembling a 1992 Chevy wasn't Megan's idea of a hobby, but then she didn't have much to say on the subject of father-daughter bonding.

So they'd agreed to meet first thing in the morning, at the park. Of course, first thing had meant after the medical timer, breakfast, and the multi-colored pills.

The park was on the small side, but it was only a few blocks from Megan's house and had a playground with a slide. That also meant it typically had enough mothers with small children nearby that Megan's mother didn't mind her hanging out there. As they got older, and some of the neighborhood kids started getting their drivers' licenses, most of the locals started traveling further to where there was more space for actual sports, or at least fewer small children, but it had continued to serve as the favored meeting spot for the girls for now.

And now it was time to discuss... a lot. Most prominent on the agenda was the crow-and-Painted-Lady thing, although that seemed even more surreal and impossible right now than it had as it happened.

Despite the obviousness of the looming questions about tiny ladies with tattered wings talking to crows, Lani had some questions of her own first before she let Megan get a word in edgewise. "How are you doing?"

"Okay," Megan answered. "A little headachey. Wondering if it's some kind of hallucination headache, considering."

"That would be a no. It's probably more of a...well, a readjustment-to-a-more-appropriate-dosage headache."

"Huh? Haven't changed my dosage in weeks."

"Well—and I'm sorry about this, and I want to apologize for that right off—you did, recently. The orange pills in your room right now are just Vitamin C."

"Okay, that really doesn't seem like a thing that should happen. At all."

"I know, and I'm sorry. I just couldn't think of what else to do, and it's an emergency."

"Okay. Apology accepted. And I could probably use a little extra Vitamin C. So, now that we've been mature about that, for certain values of mature, I guess it's time to talk about…little winged people?"

"Definitely time to discuss little winged people, and a lot of other people you'd probably find even stranger," Lani agreed.

"Let's start with the butterfly and the crow. Then we'll hit weirder."

"You're usually the one who loves the weird."

"Today is definitely not usual. So, butterfly and crow. Not hallucinating due to my best friend replacing the pills my mom worked so hard to get for Vitamin C tablets?"

"I said I was sorry."

"And the apology was accepted. I'm not upset. I'm just saying that seems like a far more likely reason for… things."

"No. Not hallucinating. The butterfly is actually a pixie. Her name is Ashling. And technically, she's the one who replaced your orange pills for Vitamin C tablets."

"Only when it was your idea, though, right?" Lani was the one who had apologized for it, after all. "She's not going to go doing anything else odd?"

"Probably not," Lani replied, not sounding at all certain. "The vitamin C thing was all I asked for."

"And she was the one who left my window open, or did she have help?"

"No, that was her."

"How?"

"So first you think you're hallucinating, now you're debating the physics of pixies?"

"I wasn't even aware physics applied to pixies, because, you know, no such thing as pixies."

"Shh, you'll hurt her feelings."

Megan looked around, not seeing any signs of a butterfly, though there were some crows not far away, but that was normal. "So she's listening?"

"Probably not," Lani replied, with the same uncertain tone. "Sneaking around is sometimes something they do, but she usually doesn't bother. Most people can't see her anyway."

"So now she's your invisible friend? But totally real?"

"You're being unusually difficult about this."

"I think I'm being really, really easy about this, considering you just told me that your invisible friend snuck in through my window in order to steal my medication, before riding off into the night on her black steed."

"Now you're just having fun with me."

"Actually, yes," Megan admitted, finally breaking into a small grin. "Now spill. Pixies."

Lani sighed. "Okay, one, it's good to have you back—"

"This is neither your weird cult of engineering, nor math class. Stop counting. Pixies."

"Right. So Ashling is a faerie, specifically, a pixie. Most people can only see her as a butterfly. It's not so much that she changes shape as that the majority of people's minds just fill in what they're seeing with something they can accept. Most faeries are like that."

"So why was I able to see her?"

"Two reasons. First, at dawn and dusk, it gets easier. Some people can kind of see them, but just ignore it. Others can see, and then, usually a few seconds later, they blink, look again, see what they expect, and forget it."

"And the other reason?"

"Well, some people, assuming they're not in an overdosed haze, have a bit of an edge at seeing something from Faerie as what it is." Lani took a breath, looking slightly sheepish. "And that's getting into family stuff."

"Family stu—" but Lani cut Megan off.

"Megan, come on, we need to go! Now!" Lani insisted, grabbing for Megan's arm.

At first, Megan didn't move when the shorter girl started tugging, looking around for the source of the alarm. There were people around the park, a couple of joggers, a lady walking her dog, and a guy walking from the play field with a bat in hand, but nothing looked immediately threatening. "What?"

Lani pointed frantically at the man with the bat and a red '49ers baseball cap. "We need to go. Run!" she insisted.

Megan's brain caught up with the words and the pointing. The guy with the cap was walking casually, but definitely moving towards them. That realization hit at the same point as she remembered that the park really wasn't big enough for baseball. Trusting in Lani's judgment amid all of the sudden weird declarations, she turned to follow her into a sprint. Megan's first glance back over her shoulder confirmed that as soon as he knew he'd been noticed, with the girls off at a run, the man in the cap was giving chase.

"Lani, what?"

"Redcap. Don't let him catch you!" Lani called back, as the pair picked up speed. Both the girls and the guy giving chase ignored the shouts of the others in the park as they took notice.

"A what?" Megan managed between breaths, keeping up with Lani, if barely. She had the longer legs, but wasn't in as good a condition.

"Less talk, more running!" Lani shouted back, reaching the edge of the park and looking around before picking a direction and tearing uphill as fast as she could.

"Where... going?" Megan called, falling a little further behind as they hit the steep hill.

"Don't look back. Run," Lani called, before adding, "Bus."

"Bus?" Megan tried, clutching her own hat and attempting to catch back up.

"Bus," Lani said determinedly, turning another corner at the end of the block. She cut across the street as soon as there was a lull in traffic. A couple of horns blared as Megan charged after her, but she got across the street without getting hit. A glance back that she couldn't quite help revealed the man in the cap looking around at first, then noticing the sound of the horns and picking up his pace again, gaining on them despite the delay.

"Cops?" Megan shouted at Lani, now several feet ahead of her, trying to fish for her phone while she ran.

"Won't help. Run!" Lani shouted back. Another glance back, and the man in the cap was closer still.

Megan saw the bus pulling up at the other end of the block, took a deep breath, and tried to just put her head down and sprint, hoping the driver would see them. She was stopped short when a hand closed around her arm. She tried to pull away, but the grip was like a vise, tightening enough to hurt.

"Megan!" called Lani, turning and starting to run back, before she got a good look at the person holding Megan's arm and paused, frozen in her tracks with a look of terror on her face.

Megan looked back. Unnaturally yellow eyes peered out from under the cap, and though she still mostly saw a person, the man's grin just kept widening, and she would swear he had at least four rows of teeth, each set in worse need of dental care than the last. She got an impression of the baseball bat being lifted. At the close-up look, despite her brain screaming at her to keep fighting, Megan froze, finding her limbs refusing to respond to her urging.

There was a whispering of wind through the trees, and a black shape dove at the man's eyes, knocking the cap to the ground. As he let go of Megan, his jagged fingernails raked at her arm, tearing right through her winter jacket and leaving bloodstained streaks before he stumbled away, covering his eyes.

Lani broke free of the trance first. "Megan, run!"

Not needing to be told twice, Megan shook off the paralysis and sprinted after Lani, adrenaline pushing until she not only caught up, but reached the bus first.

"Ashling won't distract him long," Lani huffed, trying to push Megan onto the bus faster. "Don't look," she added quickly, before Megan could glance out the opposite window.

Lani quickly fished bus fare out of her pocket. The driver, either having seen the chase, or just having waited long enough, pulled away before she'd even finished counting out the right amount. As they stumbled towards a seat, Megan glanced back to see a crow with an oddly colorful decoration on his back flying upward, away from the man with the bat. The man glared after the bus for a few moments, sending a shiver up Megan's spine even from that distance. By the time she pulled her gaze away, he was reaching for his cap.

When Megan turned her eyes back to Lani, her friend was looking worriedly at her arm, reaching for it for a closer inspection. Megan lifted her arm and rolled her sleeve up, glancing at the shallow cuts. "We'll need to clean it out really good. I don't even want to know what was under his nails. But it's not bad," Megan tried, attempting to sound reassuring.

"No, no. It's really bad," Lani replied, staring at the cuts, and going through her pockets to try to find something to wipe at the blood with. "At least we have a head start."

"We could get off anywhere," Megan replied. "Don't tell me he can magically run after the bus or something."

"He won't need to," Lani replied grimly. "He's gotten a taste of you. He can follow you anywhere. Wherever we get off, he won't be far behind."

"Why can't we call the cops? Or your Mom. She knows about this stuff too, doesn't she?"

"Look, it's complicated. Yes, she knows, but she's not going to know what to do about a redcap."

"And the pixie can't help? She has weird stuff too, right?"

"If there were ten of her, he wouldn't come anywhere near us. With just one, she delayed him a little, and even that was brave. Most pixies wouldn't try, and even fewer crows. Redcaps are... well, really bad news."

"I'm getting that impression. So he can follow us anywhere, he runs faster than I do, and we don't have any magic on our side that will stop him?"

"I told you there were matters of life and death! I just didn't expect a redcap. At least not already. Someone is moving fast."

"The redcap," Megan agreed.

"Really, really complicated," Lani assured her. "I might just know one place we can go, though. If I'm remembering the day right, if nothing else happened, if... well, let's just say there's a lot of Ifs."

"I'm getting that impression," Megan deadpanned. "So where are we going?"

"By the stadiums. Catch your breath, cross your fingers, and get ready to get off the bus running. This will be close."

Chapter 5: Busker

Megan had a few thousand more questions start to form in her head as they rode, but each one disappeared into thoughts of those eyes, those teeth, and trying to ready herself to run. To run for where, she wasn't sure, but at least she knew the area around the stadium. A lot of her mother's clients held their events in the area, or, for the really big deals, at the stadiums themselves. While her mother never attended shows, she'd ended up bringing Megan along to meetings at times.

Even more familiarity came from the Kahales, die-hard football fans, bringing her along to games. Megan liked them. That had less to do with the football and more to do with the excitement and activity, but she kept track of the Seahawks anyway, and the hat Mr. Kahale had bought her at her first game had become a constant of her wardrobe.

Lani left the bus running, with Megan right behind her. Not seeing the redcap was almost worse than if she saw him right behind them. From the moment they were off the bus, Megan was sure she was seeing flashes of the red hat in every group of people and around every corner. She tried to focus straight ahead and just not lose track of Lani.

She would normally never attempt to run on the steep, winding pathways leading down to Safeco Field, especially in the middle of the day, with so many people around. The girls got a lot of angry shouts and calls to slow down, but both ignored them. Lani had an easier time avoiding people, ducking around them. Occasionally the shorter girl leading the way made people at least watch for anyone else running at them, but Megan still ended up ricocheting off a few people, shouting "Sorry!" backwards without breaking stride.

At last she saw him as they were approaching a long stairway and a bank of elevators. He was still some way away, trailing the pair, but Megan was well aware both how quickly he could cover ground, and that if she wasn't careful, she'd end up transfixed again. She tore her gaze away and just focused on Lani as her friend rushed for the stairs.

At the bottom of the stairs, there was more foot traffic, but spaced out in the wide area around the base of the stadium. A saxophone player stood near one of the support columns, her instrument case open next to her. Megan took the stairs two at a time, trying her best to keep up speed without losing her balance. At the bottom, however, Lani grabbed her arm. Megan's first instinct on being grabbed was to try to fight free, but seeing who it was, she stopped, looking at Lani in confusion.

Despite the dire situation, Lani seemed much more relaxed than she had been on the bus. "Can I borrow a dollar?"

"What?" Megan was getting some kind of psychological whiplash.

"Can I borrow a dollar?" Lani repeated, looking at the bronze-skinned 20-something woman with the saxophone and the open case.

"I'm still a teensy bit bleeding. You said he 'has a taste' for me now and will be anywhere we go, and you ..."

"Could really stand to borrow a dollar, yeah."

Megan silently reached into her pocket and pulled out a dollar.

"Thanks," Lani replied, before, with an odd calm, going over and putting it in the saxophone case, as if that was a thing that one did after running for one's life from a monster/'49ers fan. She returned to Megan's side quickly and weathered the confounded staring well.

It took Megan a moment to process what song the saxophone started playing. It would have been difficult even had she not been standing outside with blood staining her torn sleeve and panic fueling her pulse. She'd certainly heard it plenty of times. She just wasn't used to hearing it as a simple melody on the saxophone. She was used to hearing old ladies with guitars, blaring from Lani's stereo—and the voice of every single Kahale present in the house singing along. It wasn't some perfect four-part harmony or anything, but Lani's parents—if her Dad was in town—and her little brother always sang along warmly.

"Okay. First, how did you—wait, no. First, why aren't we running anymore? Second, what the hell is going on? Now, third: how did you find the only busker in the world who knows your crazy engineering folk song?"

"He knows it's not worth it anymore. And I promise I'll explain. Now please give me a minute. We need a moment to settle, and this is a classic."

Megan sighed and waited, listening since she didn't have another option. At least the song was, admittedly, a better focus for her attention than the stinging of her arm and the memory of those eyes. She knew every word, including all the technical ones she didn't actually know. She didn't get it. It wasn't just that she wasn't the right kind of nerd to identify as much with a song comparing people to construction materials. It was that no song brought Megan and her mother together the way this song centered the Kahales together. Megan's mother rarely sang along to the radio at all, and when she started to, she never finished. It was yet another of the Kahales' Family Things—entertainment, holiday collaborations, projects—that Megan didn't have.

As the song ended, Lani took a breath. "Okay. Time to meet her."

Lani led the way up to the woman with the saxophone. She was taller than either of the girls—admittedly, most people were taller than Lani. She was also a lot more athletic, judging by the muscle tone in her arms—the fact the woman seemed comfortable in just a t-shirt in the cold weather also struck Megan as odd. The t-shirt was some kind of band shirt, with Bauhausish letters reading 'Sax & Violins.' Megan wondered if the woman and her string-playing compatriot had formed a band just for the name. Then she realized that was an odd train of thought for a time like this, but then, that had been the norm for Megan until the past month.

Stranger still, before bothering to say hi to the woman that she clearly knew, Lani was crouching over the saxophone case. Two little heads rose to greet her—a pair of little tan-with-black-spots kittens. The similar coloration and patterns suggested they were siblings, but differentiating the pair was made easy by the fact that the one on the right was wearing a little leather helmet with cutouts for his ears and a pair of goggles. Despite everything else that had happened through the day, Megan couldn't help but stare. "That's... really weird," she muttered.

"Sure is," the busker agreed. "But Maxwell insists on riding without a helmet." She gestured to a Vespa parked some way away, with a basket on the front. "He's crazy."

Megan wasn't sure, from a distance, as she looked at the human-sized safety helmet hanging off of the Vespa. "Are there... two holes drilled into yours?"

"Yep," said the saxophonist. "Matter of comfort," she added, as if that explained anything.

Lani stood upright after greeting the kittens, rolling her eyes. "Megan, meet Cassia."

Megan paused, eyeing the woman, and then looking around for the redcap. "You're sure he's not going to just follow us more?"

"Not while we stay with Cassia," Lani answered confidently.

"So she's another one of the faerie things?" Megan asked, without near as much confidence.

"A satyress," Cassia responded. "You think I'm hot now, just wait 'til dusk, and it'll be all horns and hooves."

"So, he's afraid of her?" Megan ventured.

"Most of the time, they'd probably both enjoy the fight," Lani replied. "Right now, though, it's three on one. Even a redcap isn't going to like those odds."

"Because we were so useful before." Megan snorted.

"Oh no, not us. Them." Lani gestured to the saxophone case.

"He's afraid of kittens?" Megan asked, taking a closer look at the pair.

"If you haven't figured this out, yet," Lani began, "You can't trust how Faerie things look on this side. Anyway, Cassia, can we come home with you?"

"I owe the old man enough," Cassia said. "About time I paid some more of it off. Come on." She headed for her case and the kittens, both of whom were almost standing, front paws on the sides of the case, glaring in the direction the redcap had last been seen in.

"Right, nothing is what is seems. Got it." Megan reached down to scritch one of the apparently very scary kittens in thanks.

Chapter 6: Family Stuff

Cassia tailed their next bus to Fremont closely, then rejoined them as they passed various photography galleries, rows of new condos, and what they were assured was a very nice vegan and gluten-free bakery.

Cassia showed them to her apartment, which consisted of the second floor of a house that looked like it had been built in the 1920s.

"Nice flag," Lani said, looking at the rainbow flag hanging from Cassia's balcony.

"Thanks. Fits in nice in this neighborhood, and of course, I am pansexual."

Megan had heard that word. "Ah, right. Attraction that doesn't specify any physical sex or gender identity, right?"

"Yeah. Besides, Pan is really hot."

Megan blinked. "...Okay."

Cassia just smiled, let them into her place, took a letter opener out of her coat and set it on the front table. Why the busker carried around a letter opener was added to an incredibly long list of unanswered questions. Megan wasn't sure she'd ever have time for all of them.

"Is that a Richard Dadd?" Megan asked, eyes immediately drawn to the chaotic painting in Cassia's living room.

"Just a print, obviously, but yeah," Cassia confirmed. "Crazy Jane. I love it. Love the Yeats poems it helped inspire, too. *'Fair and foul are near of kin/And fair needs foul,'* I cried. Good stuff."

"I've seen some of Dadd's work with the ...faeries. Did he paint this in the asylum too?"

"Yep. Most of his best work there."

Megan frowned. "Are you going to tell me that he wasn't really crazy? That he met actual faeries?"

"Oh, he was definitely really crazy. Severe paranoid schizophrenia. Horrific violent delusions." Cassia smiled, a little disturbing, considering the subject. "That absolutely does not mean he never met any real faeries." The taller woman sprawled on her couch. The kittens, Jude and Maxwell, bounded across the floor before climbing up onto the couch with their owner. "So, you're Megan O'Reilly,"

"Yeah, um, how much do you know about me?"

"You as the menehune's BFF, or you as Riocard's daughter with the frontwoman of Late to the Party?"

Well, that opened up a whole new game of questions. Megan knew her parents had been in a band when she was born, much as her mom didn't like to talk about parts of her life she'd 'grown out of.' But Megan had always assumed Ric was short for Richard. Still, there was an even more urgent issue. "Minnie-what?" She looked to Lani.

"Menehune. And only half. I'm human on my mom's side."

"Human on your ..." Megan frowned. "Lani, I've met your dad. He's a person."

"A person, yeah," Lani said. "That's a reasonable label. Not human. And you've never seen Dad at dusk, and definitely never at dawn." Upon reflection, Megan hadn't. Lani's dad was away for work a lot, though, so it never seemed weird to not see him in the evening much.

While she was reflecting, she repeated the word. "Menehune." Megan remembered where she heard the term before. "Wait ... the Hawaiian lawn gnome people? Like your mom's old figurine thing on top of the fridge? Your dad's not ..." Well, if pressed, she had to admit the figurine looked a bit like him. And it was a little harder to call this entire conversation insane considering her conversation of the night before. "But he works for the Corps of Engineers!" she protested lamely.

"Did I ever say which Corps of Engineers?"

"...No," Megan said slowly, reproachfully. "You didn't."

"Megan, I wanted to tell you. I always wanted to tell you. But there are Restrictions."

Megan could hear the capitalization in Lani's voice. She'd heard it before from the Kahales about cultural stuff, like really strong kinda-sorta-religious principles against overfishing. It only helped a little. "Okay. So why are you telling me now? Why get disabled butterfly-people with service-crows to say we need to talk about what you couldn't say during fifty sleepovers? When did it stop being Restricted?"

"Last week," Lani answered quietly. "When I found out you're only human on your mom's side, too."

Megan paused for some time. "Okay, before I can either laugh or scream about that, I'm going to need a sandwich and some Band-Aids."

Despite being the technical hostess, Cassia remained sprawled out on her couch, with a pair of kittens climbing on her. The satyress gestured towards the kitchen. "Feel free."

"I've got it," Lani replied, heading for the apartment's small kitchen at the invitation, peeking out to continue the conversation while she prepared food for herself and Megan.

"So," Cassia asked suddenly. "What do you play?"

"What?" Megan was getting whiplash again. A hand went to her hat. "Just a fan. Don't play sports."

"Not sports. Music. What instrument? Your mother's bass work was incendiary. My girl—" Cassia gestured to a picture of herself with arm around a dreadlocked woman holding a violin bow. "—still plays those albums. So what about you?"

"Oh. Keyboards, like, a little. Music class is always fun. I have perfect pitch, Ms. Dahl says..."

"Well, yeah," Cassia said, shrugging, and Megan wondered if the perfect pitch was somehow related to not being human. The satyress continued. "But seriously, just 'keyboards, a little'?" She sighed, then muttered. "Ric, you and your attachment issues have a lot to answer for."

Megan wasn't sure she was ready to ask after that yet. "So what's a redcap?"

"Very violent Unseelie." Lani replied from the other side of the kitchen counter.

"Un-what?"

"Disorderly fairies. There's these two courts for the Irish and British types and anyone associated with them: Seelie and Unseelie.

We're Seelie, my family. Well, we're affiliated with the Seelie Court. Because of the Menehune-Brownie Strategic Alliance of 1801."

"...obviously. And what do Irish and British fairies have to do with Seattle?"

"You think colonization is just a human thing? For one thing, there's dandelions—but best not to get us off track."

"Yeah... That used to be my job," said Megan.

Lani smiled. "Yeah. Anyway, it's all very complicated, but a lot of connections lead a lot of different places, and a lot of various Folk end up where they want to end up—"

"But some things are always going to be Irish," Cassia said. "Because Riocard has a Type."

"So you knew my dad?" Megan asked her.

"Sure. Still see him twice a year, except when I don't feel like going."

"And you're saying he's... a faerie? Like..."

"Not like Ashling," Lani said hurriedly.

Cassia laughed. "Ooh, no, not like Ashling."

"He's one of the sidhe," Lani continued. "The highest order of the Irish and British faeries. He's one of the top among even the sidhe, really. Sometimes he goes by the Unseelie King."

"Wait, what? My dad is Unseelie? Like the redcap? Does... does he—?"

Cassia stepped in. "No, trust me, he didn't send that guy. Just because they're both Unseelie doesn't make them allies. Really, that thing about keeping friends close and so on can kind of apply. Now, some of us—"

"Us?" Megan interjected.

"Us," Cassia assured. "I fell in with Ric's folk a long time ago. Came along his first road trip to America—not that this continent had much in the way of roads at the time. My folk ain't always so big on letting me play reindeer games anymore, but I like the local Unseelie, messed up as some of 'em are, and I like Seattle."

"Well...yeah," Megan said. "Seattle's great. Attracts...all kinds of people."

Chapter 7: Seasons of Change

"So..." Megan asked, finishing a bite of the sandwich Lani made her and occasionally wincing at the disinfectant being applied to her arm. "My dad is what, '80s David Bowie? Glammed up, stealing babies, turning into owls?"

Lani frowned. "*Sort* of, but don't get me started on owls."

"What is your problem with owls?"

"I'm not *scared* of them, to be clear. I'm a big girl. I just think they're up to something"

"Okay, okay, forget the owls."

"Gladly."

"So aside from something about attachment issues with the father I've never met, exactly what's going on? Why would someone want to kill me?"

"I'll take this one," Cassia said. "Faerie is all about politics and schemes. Bad blood can last a lot of centuries, and your dad is one of the major players. He's done a hell of a job hiding you all these years, particularly after he managed to spend four years with your mom. The people who knew were either actual allies, or weren't willing to cross him. Now that he's missing, somebody also leaked word on who you are and where you are. As word gets out, plenty of people want to meet you—and at least a few others are just as interested in making sure you're not around to meet. The redcap may just be the start."

Despite the threat to her life, Megan fixated on another part of the explanation. "My dad is missing? Like, missing from, uhm, Faerie, missing?"

"That's what I've been trying to tell you," Lani said. "I got some advance notice from Ashling, but not much. I knew it wouldn't take long for more people to find out."

"How did Ashling find out?"

"After the thing with her wings," Cassia said, "Riocard took her in. She's been his hunting guide for a while, when he's not sending her to keep an eye on you."

Megan scratched her head. "I'm having trouble keeping track of who is on what team here."

Lani applied a little more disinfectant and started bandaging Megan's arm. "It's not always about teams. My dad might disagree with him a lot of the time, but it's absolutely critical that we find your dad before Halloween and get him back where he's supposed to be."

"So he's … he's not even on your team. You're just worried because he's my dad?"

"Not just. I want you in on this because it's important, and you deserve to know. But just because we're not affiliated with the Unseelie doesn't mean they're not important. If I've learned anything from Neil deGrasse Tyson, it's that without Autumn, we'd all freeze to death."

"How are you trying to use science geek stuff to explain to me that… that we're faeries?"

"Well, we're only half. Anyway, my point is that there are sort of … mystic-climate patterns and stuff, and they're all part of what keeps back the kinda-sorta Ice Age. Getting your dad back is important besides his being your dad."

"Okay, so one more time, mystic climate patterns?"

Cassia sighed. "Riocard and Orlaith both take turns ruling things. The Seelie Queen in mostly Spring and Summer, your dad from Halloween to May Day. Lots of other faeries all over the world have their own things, but any one of them can screw things up. Your dad not taking over when he's supposed to is one of those screw-ups."

"So what do I have to do with it? Sure, he's my dad, but if it's that bad, there has to be plenty of people trying to find him with a lot more tricks and stuff than I'd have. I barely remember him."

"The Seelie Queen says there's a possible way to safely retrieve him, but that it needs someone of human blood," Lani says. "And I've got Restrictions; I can help in stuff like that, but I can't do it alone."

"Meanwhile, the Unseelie ain't exactly known for their teamwork," Cassia said. "There's some folks looking for Ric, sure, but I suspect most don't have a clue, and the ones who do, I don't trust."

"So what are we supposed to do, exactly?"

"Well, first, Ashling and the Count know more than just about anyone, so we have a lead. Then we'll go to the courts, talk to the Queen. Ashling also says she was told to find you, so if you can believe her, your dad thinks there's something you can do."

"If you can believe her?"

"Pixies have a rep. She's more reliable than most."

"Well, that's comforting. I guess. So what do I need to do?"

"We're still waiting on a couple of people who should be here soon. We'll need Ashling's help in Faerie, and Kerr is on the way."

"So we're going to Faerie? Like, another world?"

"That's right."

"Uhm, I get that this is world-threatening stuff and all, but with going to another world—how long is this going to take?"

"Getting there doesn't take long at all." Cassia said. "Having Ashling along will speed things up too. But the trip is only half the trick. Figuring out what happened, where Ric is, and getting to him will probably take a few days, at least. If not longer."

"What? I can't stay the night. It's hard enough getting Mom to let me stay at Lani's house."

"I know," Lani said. "That's why I've called in the other friend I mentioned." She looked to the door, and it opened. Someone came in, someone shorter than Lani, with a wide, ruddy face and tawny hair, dressed in baggy beige clothes and a knit cap. Lani smiled. "Right on cue, as usual. Thanks for making the trip on short notice, Kerr," Lani said, raising her hand in the shape of the 'okay' sign, then tapping just above her eye and waving, like a little salute. The new arrival returned the gesture. It looked almost like a secret handshake. Lani had secret handshakes with other people, about whom her BFF knew nothing. Megan didn't know how to feel about that.

"Megan, I'd like you to meet Kerr."

"Nice to meet you, Megan," Kerr said in warm, friendly voice that was either tenor or alto, with an awkward little movement that was sort of a curtsey-ish bow. All of Kerr's features were a little hard to place as Megan smiled and managed an actual handshake. Why couldn't everyone come with little notes to identify what pronoun you were supposed to use for them, like on Tumblr?

"Nice to meet you, too. So, you're....?"

"A brownie."

"Ah. Right. Strategic alliances and all."

"Yep. I'm here to smooth things over at home for you. What's the plan?"

"Ms. O'Reilly needs to think Megan's home by supper," Lani said. "She can be 'in her room' outside of meals. If we're not back by Monday, the math homework needs to be turned in at school. Megan needs to be seen so no one calls her mom, but 'she' can turn in mine while I'm sick."

The brownie was nodding. Megan couldn't believe they were having this conversation, of course. Most high school students did not get a personal assistant. But if they were going to have it, best to go for the best. "And some of the equations might need checking."

"Will do." And there was that okay-salute again, and the bow-curtsey again, and Kerr was scurrying out.

Everything she was experiencing brought more questions to Megan's mind, so she continued just asking the first ones to spring to mind. "How did... Kerr... do that? Just sort of showing up when you mentioned... Kerr?" Megan asked, at a loss for pronouns.

"Brownies are very good at being right on time. Also very good with the little household magics and a few illusions. Your mom won't notice a thing, and we'll get you back as soon as we can."

"Survival permitting," Cassia muttered to the kittens, just before the one with the aviator helmet was pounced by his brother.

Megan didn't like the sound of that, including the thought there might be a lot more redcaps, or worse, where the one came from. She was interrupted from this reflection when the playful wrestling of kittens turned into something from a nature documentary, with two adult-sized leopards leaping and tussling. As Megan squeaked and dove from the sofa, she saw the light of dusk filtering in and shining on goat-like horns curving out of Cassia's thick black hair.

Suddenly, moments after the world went crazy, everything returned to the way it had seemed. Megan got back up and dusted herself off as Cassia grinned. "Told you."

Megan sat down again in surreal normality, trying not to give Cassia anything to encourage her playful gloating. Instead, she turned to Lani, trying to go through which questions came to mind that didn't involve how, if the kittens were really leopards, they weren't knocking things over left and right. "Before anything more, where'd the word Seelie come from, anyway?"

"It's an old word for punctual," piped a voice from out on the balcony. The crow was perched there, and the amber-skinned little Painted Lady was sitting atop him. "I'm Seelie myself," she said. "Don't listen to anyone who says different."

Chapter 8: Mazes of Words ... and Ice

"Where did you come from?" Megan asked, immediately feeling stupid.

"Originally? Evolved from baby's laughter, obviously. Just now? We've been leading a merry chase that wasn't very merry."

"Right. Thanks. So ... what happened to my father? They said you know more."

"He went hunting..." Ashling started. There followed a long stretch of explanations of hunting in Faerie, fantastic beasts that Megan had to admit might be possible in Faerie, or might be Ashling exaggeration. Most likely, she figured, there was some combination of all of the above.

She listened to the meandering as best she could manage, until Ashling mentioned her father again. "...he does this a lot, when he's in Faerie. My cousin Nessa calls it his safari streak. There's a big dance that follows The Dance, and then a feast. The King likes to provide a new trophy every year as the centerpiece-slash-entree for the feast. Well, except some years, like the years with your mom, or the year he did a tour of all the castles of Scotland for nostalgia's sake, or the year he tried to invade Sweden..."

Somewhere in the list of Riocard's adventures, Megan found herself staring at the torn sections of each of Ashling's wings, then trying to analyze what exact shade of pink was on their underside, before the story cycled back around.

"...there was plenty of time. So he had me guide him out into the mountains. He knows them pretty well, but the Count and I fly all over the place and had scouted it out for him. I—I guess I missed something. We thought we'd found a cave where he could get his Ellén Trechend—"

"Wait," Megan interrupted. "He was hunting *who*?"

"Not who. What. Your dad doesn't hunt people."

Megan's shoulders relaxed.

"He doesn't have the palate for it. This was for a feast, after all. An Ellén Trechend is a giant three-headed scaly-red bird-monster."'

"Oh." Megan paused. "So you thought you'd found it ..."

"Yes! We thought we'd found it. So he went in to explore. He had the Count and me cycle around to make sure there was no back way out. Then suddenly the wind carries a message from him. Something about being ambushed and trapped, telling me to run and hide, then nothing. I go back later, really sneaky, to explore. When we first found it, it hadn't looked that deep. Now, there was all sorts of passages, and even though the handover in power hadn't happened yet, it was all like an ice cave. Mirrored surfaces everywhere, and all twisty like a maze. I didn't go in very deep, so I didn't get lost. Besides, I figured there was something worse in there, since Riocard normally wouldn't have any problems with ice and cold things. That's his favorite magic."

Megan followed the last bits. "Okay, so we need to go to the caves and figure out how to find him. And figure out who ambushed him? If he's even alive. I mean, if he just stopped there."

"No, no. That wasn't the last I heard from him. There I was, turning the Count out of the cave because I didn't know the depths, didn't have a special knack for ice, and didn't see a thing except that one will o' wisp—"

"A what?" Megan had heard the term, but wasn't exactly sure how it applied here.

"Sort of like faeries, since they were also spawned from the sparks from the fire of the first storyteller..."

"I thought you said faeries came from baby's laughter."

"That's silly. Faeries were around way before there were babies."

"So the first storyteller was never a baby?"

"See, now you're asking the important questions. And that's a very good story, actually. Want to hear it?"

"Later, maybe. We're talking about my da—what's a will o' wisp again?"

"Okay, so will o' wisps are sort of like really minor faerie things, or lights that like to hang around faeries, because they eat emotions, and faeries are a constant buffet that won't wear down easy. Now and then, one or two wander through the portals and get hungry. That's where you get stories of people seeing lights in the woods and getting scared and stuff. Poor will o' wisps, they're just lost and hungry. I try to lead them back when I can." Ashling wiped a non-existent tear from her cheek, before getting back on topic. "...Where was I?"

"The cave shouldn't have scared my dad, so something more awful must have been there."

"Right! So there I was, ready to go for help, when I hear just a whisper on the wind—it's a very distinctive whisper, you see. He tells me he was betrayed and trapped, and don't trust anyone. I guess someone knew he wouldn't worry about the ice and would just get curious, and then they trapped him somewhere in the mountains. He assured me he was still alive, but faerie magic wouldn't free him. And I was supposed to go find you and bring you to Faerie."

Megan took that all in, the comments on very distinctive whispers reminding her of that voice, the one she just knew belonged to the man in the photo. The trip was obviously dangerous, but if there was any chance of it being true, she resolved to try. "You mentioned something about a dance?"

"Not so much a dance as The Dance," Lani said, before Ashling could get going on a new tale. The pixie harumphed again, but let Lani continue. "Riocard and Queen Orlaith meet and do an old, formal dance twice each year, Halloween and May Day. It rekeys all the pathways, helps keep the seasons in order—for part of the world, anyway—and helps keep some really important things in order in Faerie, too."

"Okay, so now that brings up more questions. Pathways? Who benefits from this not happening? If a faerie lord's magic can't free him, what are we supposed to do?"

Lani continued talking over Ashling, with the pixie eventually ceasing to try, and just sticking her tongue out at Lani instead. "There's various paths and shortcuts, some obvious, some hidden, between Earth and Faerie, and a lot of the different fae realms. Pixies are especially good at finding them, knowing which one leads where, and navigating them."

The compliment seemed to mollify Ashling a bit, while Lani continued. "When The Dance happens, a lot of them close, others just get more treacherous. But it's sort of a rest for the Faerie realm, though it still lets some of the nasty things wander unchecked. So there's one question."

Megan nodded, restraining herself from asking any more before Lani caught up. "Okay, so next," Lani said, "There's too many people who might benefit. Some of the Unseelie would do things just for the chaos. Some of them would also love to take Riocard's position, no matter the cost. There's plenty of intelligent and powerful creatures out there that would love to see the pathways stay open all the time, and all of the magic protecting them start to break down. We need more information."

Megan sighed. This wasn't getting any easier or any clearer, even with the explanations. Mostly, they just raised more questions.

"Finally, he wanted you in Faerie. Maybe he was just worried about sudden redcap incursions because you might not be a secret anymore, but maybe he thought you could help. Meanwhile, the Queen thinks someone of human blood can help. Great minds might have thought alike, so we're taking you to Faerie and starting at the towers. Speaking of which, tomorrow is going to be a really long day, and it's getting late. Ashling is going to lead us to the quickest path first thing tomorrow. Cassia's girlfriend should be home around 3, so there'll be at least one interruption. We should try to get some sleep while we can. Seeing Faerie tomorrow will explain a lot of things better than I could now."

"Yeah, good luck with getting to sleep," Megan said, but tried to settle in on Cassia's couch anyway, while Lani curled up in a loveseat. "Good night, Lani."

Megan's head was whirling while she tried to get comfortable. Amidst all of the wondering about faerie courts, the existence of magic, what, exactly, that meant for her, her mother's state of mind, and so many other things, she also realized she'd forgotten to ask anyone to get her medication. Not the Vitamin C that had replaced what only one out of four doctors had recommended, but the pills that four out of four doctors thought helped her function.

Oh, well. She had bigger problems now.

Chapter 9: Into Faerie

Ashling's way to the nearest passage turned out to require a trip to Fremont Peak Park. The small group navigated the gravel paths that wound through the park, and then the crow and pixie led them out onto the grass and through some of the shrubbery to a spot that would be hidden from the view of most casual passers-by.

"So, you did promise. Why's he called Count?" Megan asked, while Ashling was moving about the ground, amidst a ring of mushrooms mostly hidden under the brush and grass.

"Dressed in black, with a widow's peak," Ashling began.

How matters of hairstyle could be applied to a bird was, technically, a question that Megan could have asked, but she just stood and watched and listened as Ashling walked in a figure-8, still talking at a mile a minute.

"—and of course my cousin Nessa has told him that it's a shame he's not named the Marquis because he travels the far reaches and all, but considering his fondness for Monte Cristo sandwiches..."

Megan was seeing by now what Lani had meant about pixies, so she directed her next question to Lani. "So, it's not dawn or dusk. Why am I not seeing a butterfly?"

"It will start happening more and more. You know what she really looks like, you've accepted that pixies exist, and you're starting to acknowledge the sidhe blood thing."

"My dad being a faerie lord who decided to leave his magic realm and come join a rock band for a few years? That little thing?"

"Gee, when you put it that way, it almost sounds silly," Lani said, unable to entirely avoid smiling. "You're sounding more like yourself, though."

They glanced back to Ashling, who had stopped talking and stopped pacing. "Okay, ready," she said, before looking to Megan. "So, did you have any other questions? I like questions."

"I'll get back to you. So, how do we do this?"

Ashling was about to respond, but Lani interrupted. "Just step into the ring, close your eyes, and then step out again." While she explained, raising her voice just a bit, Ashling attempted to answer anyway, with some directions that sounded to Megan like they might have been lifted piecemeal from the hokey-pokey, the Macarena, and the time warp. Noticing no one being inclined to go through her dance, Ashling huffed, then stepped into the ring, followed by the Count. Both disappeared when they started to step—or, in the Count's case, hop—out of the ring. Lani went next, demonstrating on a larger scale. As she stepped back out of the ring, she too disappeared.

Megan took a deep breath, then stepped where Lani had been, careful to avoid the mushrooms, then closed her eyes, released the breath, and stepped back out, a little surprised when she kicked something crunchy-sounding that seemed almost to hook into her shoe.

When she opened her eyes, the entire world had changed. The first thing she noticed were the colors. Everything was brighter, starting with the sunlight, especially in comparison to the gray skies of Seattle in October. The light made it no warmer, but just added to the golden sheen in the air. This brought out the color in the marigolds and golden columbines that peeked from the vibrant green grass amid the chill. The golden haze of the air also matched the golden apples hanging within some of the dense expanse of trees, the apples that weren't red or yellow or green or mottled or pink.

Megan noticed the second thing very quickly, because if she hadn't, she would have fallen right into the raspberry bush rather than recover her balance. As it was, she barely managed to extricate her foot from the thicket it was ensnared in. The raspberry bushes, too, were filled with all varieties: red and black and purple and blue and yes, golden. All the fruit was large and ripe and glistening—in the cold.

Lani was waiting calmly by one of them, with the Count perched on one of her shoulders, and Ashling perched on the crow's neck. She turned at the sound of odd footsteps. Megan didn't blink, thanks to the 'preview' of the night before, but it was a better look this time. The woman behind her was still Cassia—the facial features were right, she was the right size, and she still had the Sax & Violins t-shirt. Now, however, the rest of her clothing was a distinctly more ancient Mediterranean style. She had loops of bronze-plated leather covering the top portion of her now-fuzzy-and-hooved legs, while the Vespa helmet had become a bronze and ivory helm, with holes left for her impressive, curving horns. The kittens were again full-sized adult leopards—one still wearing a leather helmet and goggles—and the Vespa she'd been wheeling beside her had become a small chariot. The letter opener had likewise transformed, leaving Cassia with a straight bronze sword on one hip. The satyress grinned, striking a pose.

"Time for showing off later. We have a lot of walking to do," Lani called.

Cassia sighed. "Spoilsport." There was a grin, though, and she set to securing the chariot to the pair of leopards, though once the apparently tame cats were strapped in, Cassia just walked alongside it.

As soon as everyone appeared ready, the Count lifted off of Lani's shoulder and began weaving through the trees, doubling back often to make sure the others didn't lose him.

For a while, Megan just marveled at the world around her. When there was sufficient breaks in the trees to see them, towering peaks that looked like they'd dwarf the Cascades—and probably the Rockies as well—loomed in the distance. There was the occasional sound of birds. More disturbing, Megan was constantly feeling like she was being watched and occasionally would swear she saw motion out of the corner of her eyes. Any time she turned her head, there was no sign of anyone but herself and her companions. The others weren't exactly relaxed, but they also weren't looking around every few seconds, so she did her best to convince herself it was her imagination, fueled by the haze of golden light, which was occasionally almost lens-flaresque.

She therefore stared straight ahead, which for the moment, was at Cassia. "Now, wait a minute," Megan said after considering for a moment. "You've got the horns, like the fauns in Etruscan and Roman art, but the outfit is Bronze Age Greece, and that—" she pointed at the horse-like tail emerging from the armored skirt. " —is an old-school Bronze Age satyr's tail." Mrs. Chang's Art History Thursdays, sophomore year, had been more fun for Megan than regular history.

"While I appreciate your checking out my ass, Megan, satyrs and fauns have been mixed up for millennia."

"Yeah, but you can't actually be both at once."

"Don't tell me what I can't do," Cassia said good-naturedly.

After the sighing and eye-rolling, there was a pause, a silence she wanted filled with something other than the shuffle of shoes—or hooves—across the vibrantly colored ground or the thought of what was on the edge of her vision. "You said something last night about attachment issues. Is that about how my mom stopped liking music because my dad left?"

"No," Cassia said. "I think she'd have still been able to heal, get another guitarist, and enjoy music just fine, if Riocard hadn't dated her for four freaking years, almost."

"That's … not that long."

"It was for him."

"What's the longest you've dated someone?"

"Going on two years now, but I'm young. And a satyr. With my girl, I've just got to be careful about how often we get to drinking. The mad revels and all. Go wild, fun times, dangerous, exhausting, etc. And then we're done with it for a bit. Break down and let it all out, you know? But the sidhe aren't like that. They're always on. Always. It's not one wild moment. Get too wrapped up in them, and you'll never just get a moment again. Not ever. There's a reason 'fae-touched' used to mean 'crazy.' Too much time with a sidhe will burn a person out."

That commentary quieted her again. She thought about the old pictures, the bass tucked away in the closet, and all of her mother's friends in the music and entertainment business, the ones who'd helped her get her job all those years ago. The ones who offered her all the free tickets that she never took. Finally, she managed, "So, my father did that to her?"

"Yes," Lani said, slowing a little to make sure she ended up beside Megan. "Not intentionally. From the bits and pieces I've heard, he really loved your mother. It's complicated, but it's something that can happen, not something he was trying to do."

"And what about your parents? How do they manage the... complicated? They've been together your whole life, and your mother seems fine."

"Menehune are a different kind of intense. They're also a lot more prone to noticing the passing of time, since they work in cycles. But even so, that's part of why my dad goes away so often, to give Mom time to just do human things, where the most menehune things going on in the house are Mack's LEGO masterpieces."

"So you do have some magic things you and Mack can do?"

"Sure. By faerie standards, it's pretty tame. We pick up languages quick, and, well, you've seen the garden, and the house. As long as we do it right, we can all build things, especially things people need. Really, my mom's hobby collection is part of why they work so well. The gardens—flower, vegetable, and rock—the pottery studio, the workout room..." she trailed off. "We're almost there."

"Almost where?" Megan said. Before she got an answer, a pale blue light zipped across the area in front of her before disappearing in the trees. Then another light zipped out of the shadows, but this one paused, hovering in mid-air in front of them. Two more emerged behind it. Looking back, Megan couldn't help but notice that Cassia had her hand on her sword.

Within a few moments, the lights weren't the only company. A dozen tiny people, similar to Ashling, but with undamaged wings, emerged to rest on the branches of the trees around them. Ashling and the Count settled on Lani's shoulder again, both making a point of looking at the floating lights, but conspicuously paying the other pixies no attention.

These arrivals were followed, on foot, by two groups. The first were knights in literally shining armor, marching in one small group. Though the armor largely hid their features, Megan could tell they were all unusually tall and slender, and while hardly silent, she was a bit surprised that they could move as quickly and quietly as they did in the full armor. The second group, Megan slowly realized, must be what redcaps really looked like. They were still very like people in many ways, but their clothing was mostly layers of rags, bearing stains she didn't even want to identify. Their faces were broad, with flat noses and bright yellow eyes. It seemed like a third of their face was grin, showing off their rows of broken and jagged teeth. Each one wore a different type of hat, but each one was mostly red, though they also bore the brownish stains of dried blood. Seeing them like this didn't help, but at least she wasn't freezing in place again.

Lani stepped forward, and one of the pale lights advanced to float a couple of feet in front of her. As it approached, Megan couldn't help but notice that, despite the light it shed, it radiated cold, instead of the slight warmth of a lantern that she'd expected. When it stopped advancing, Lani curtsied to the floating light. Cassia and the cats advanced, flanking Megan on either side. She noted that the satyr hadn't taken her hand off the sword. Megan couldn't make out the words, but though the air was still, she heard the whispering of wind through the trees, getting the idea that the pixies were chattering among themselves.

Finally, the light dimmed slightly, dipping lower as if it was bowing to Lani in return and flitting a little to take in Megan and the others as well. "The Gray Lady will see you." The voice emitted from the light, Megan was sure of it. It was slightly above a whisper, but the words were almost sung more than spoken.

"After the Queen does," one of the knights said solemnly, stepping forward.

A few of the redcaps managed the feat of rolling their eyes while grinning.

"Who is—" Megan began, before she felt Cassia's hand on her shoulder. She took the cue and quieted, just following after Lani, who was following the light as it started moving away from them through the woods. The rest of the floating lights moved to flank them, and the pixies took to flight, fluttering around the small group, sticking to the trees just a bit out of anyone's reach. The other two groups spent a few moments looking at each other, some glaring, some more subdued, and then they, too, moved to take flanking positions to escort the group. Megan couldn't tell which bunch Cassia spent more time looking at, with the same guarded expression either way.

"The knights seem a bit smug about mentioning that the Queen goes first," Megan said.

"That's just water getting wetter," Cassia said, still looking around.

Finally, the trees gave way to a wide clearing. Even half a mile away, the castle at the center was clearly visible. While she'd seen pictures of European castles in books, this was more like something out of a tale. Instead of a mere four, a dozen towers stretched into the skies. Security walls and watchtowers ringed the main building, all of it covered with climbing ivy.

"It still doesn't seem real," Megan breathed.

Lani paused, stepping back to reassure her. "It's as real as anything. They call it An Teach Deiridh: basically, The Last Home." She glanced at their multiple honor guards for a moment. "I think we're expected."

Chapter 10: The Queen and Her General

The route through the castle to the Queen was a sort of torture to Megan's attention span. The castle itself didn't appear to be so much built as carved, with most of it looking like it was made of one piece of stone. The walls were lined with artwork that ranged from paintings to ornate mirrors to more suits of the fancy armor the knights wore. Everything was laid out to catch the golden light that came streaming in through the windows, giving it a shine that gave the place the feel of a treasure horde.

Catching her even more off-guard was how alive things felt. The ivy from the walls outside continued in through the windows in many places, winding around the treasures and up the walls. The expanses of green, as they reached inside, bore sudden new flowers of various colors, dozens of varieties coming from the same plant. While most of these were similar to blooms she could identify, others appeared to be almost more crafted than grown, with petals of near-translucent gold and silver. More than once, Lani and Cassia had to help urge Megan along in the correct direction before she got drawn into her mental notes to paint one part of this scene or another.

The residents of the place were, if anything, even more striking. Some of them she recognized. Pixies and apparently related species were especially omnipresent. They mostly gathered together in large groups, whirling about in complex dances on both the ground and in the air, while similarly tiny things with cricket legs and dragonfly wings fiddled or played reed flutes. All manner of butterfly wings were colorfully represented, and the moth-like pixie-kin, though more muted, were no more sedate. Sometimes they clustered with their own varieties, but sometimes they mixed freely.

People that reminded her of Kerr, mostly short and dressed in layers with muted tones, moved about, some socializing, others cleaning or carrying food. Many of the rooms also held suitable tables for bigger folk. The sidhe—people who looked like what she could see of the knights—mostly gathered together, talking, laughing, and entertaining each other or illustrating their stories with small illusions, such as flickering lights or images of tiny dancers, summoned at the wave of a hand. In others, things she guessed might best fit the description of leprechauns drank with redcaps. These stories were considerably louder, though she did her best to ignore them, pretty sure she wanted nothing to do with the types of tales redcaps would tell. After that, she ran out of names. There were people with the features of animals. Tiny fae mingled with fae who had to hunch down to get through even the massive castle doors.

Megan noted, however, that when they ran into other gatherings in the hallways, size and space permitting, everyone moved to the side to let her guarded procession pass, or moved around them, hugging the walls, rather than trying to insist her group move. Some of the less savory-looking figures around, such as at least one redcap and a tall woman-like thing with grayish green skin and too many joints, gave the sidhe knights less-than-pleasant glances but moved aside anyway. While they were making their way along, one of the redcaps, this one in a '49ers cap, looked Megan's way, grinning and giving her a playful little salute. Megan quickly looked away from the all-too familiar figure. At least this time he let them be.

Finally they came to a stop. "This is the ballroom," the knight said, gesturing at the large doors. "The Queen will see you here."

Megan was a little taken aback by that, having assumed there would be a throne room. Despite the revelry elsewhere, the ballroom was silent aside from their footfalls. Though clearly designed to host a massive crowd, the only people present were all at the far end of the room. A raised dais held an ornate throne. The wooden structure of the grand chair seemed to grow directly out of the stone floor, winding and twisting itself into the proper shape, before expanses of gold were added. At least Megan supposed they had to be added, though she couldn't see any seams between wood and metal. Settled on a crimson cushion on the throne sat the

Queen, with one figure standing just to her right and a few attendants waiting in the wings.

Megan had never fully held with the idea that attributed the majority of human beauty to symmetry. She'd try to use meeting the Seelie Queen and seeing the small, light scars on just the right side of her face as the prime refutation of the idea, but … it didn't apply. Because there was nothing remotely human about the beauty involved. As it was, the scars took her just enough out of the uncanny valley to … Megan couldn't describe it, not even to herself. She might have to paint the thought, someday. Regardless, uncanny beauty, scarred face or not, the woman had the bearing of a ruler. The knights, along with most of Megan's company, dropped to a knee before the throne. Even Cassia and the Count bowed. Megan felt a little awkward being the last to show her respects, but dropped to one knee and lowered her head.

As for the man beside the Queen ... Megan's grandparents had taken her to church a few times, whenever she visited them in Idaho. Her mom didn't hold with it much, but she'd made a bit of effort to reconcile with her family as long as they didn't push. And so Megan had spent the occasional Sunday in St. Michael's Catholic Church, staring at a stained glass window of an armored archangel serenely stabbing some kind of devil-dragon under his feet. It was on the little medals of the archangel as the patron saint of cops, too. That, Megan immediately decided, was what this guy looked like. He seemed like he absolutely ought to be stabbing a demon or a dragon in the face, right this moment, in a calm and highly professional manner. He wasn't quite like the other sidhe about, being bigger and broader than most, but there were enough similarities, and Megan was uncertain enough about what the options were, that she decided he must at least be a close relative.

"So you're Riocard's daughter," the Queen finally said. "He did a fine job hiding you away for your protection. And now he's the one in need of aid. I can respect a dutiful child." Her voice had an almost stereo effect: where Megan recalled her father's voice being quiet and smooth, Queen Orlaith's carried, echoing off the walls, even if she didn't look to be putting much effort into projecting.

"Yes, yes, Ma'am." Megan stammered, finding it harder and harder to pull her eyes away and not get lost in some sort of odd fascination with Orlaith's features. The thought occurred that it might be something like the paralytic fear the redcap induced before, even if Orlaith didn't seem to be doing anything actively magical. She finally settled for keeping her gaze forward, but studying the intricacies of Orlaith's ornate dress, which looked to Megan like it might have been spun from spidersilk and dew drops, somehow held together with metallic platinum strands and highlights.

"Then you won't mind taking on a bit of a challenge. Dear Ashling has shared her information with me. From that, and what I've been able to deduce, Riocard is trapped in a prison warded against our magics, and likely well guarded. We will be investigating as well, as securing his release soon is critical. I also already sent one agent out to attempt to gain the only thing I'm certain could work—but we've lost track of him. Unfortunately, that quest is not one that can be completed by faerie-kind."

"And you'd like us to follow up?" Megan guessed.

"Clever girl," the Queen agreed. "The city of Findias was lost to us." At the name, she heard Cassia suck in a breath, while Lani looked a little stunned. "But it still stands, encased in iron. It was once a place of great festivals, known for its art and music, even among the Gods. Now, it stands silent as a tomb. Even so, within lies one of the greatest gifts the Gods left for human hand: the Claiomh Solais, the Sword of Light. Among its legends is the ability to bypass, or destroy, all manner of enchantments. In the right hands, it would readily melt away those chaotic walls of ice, lead a person to the enchanted prison, and allow them to free Riocard."

Megan glanced among the members of her group, with Lani and Cassia alike looking at the Queen incredulously. "So, this sword, we go to the city, get it, and we can free my dad?"

"If you should happen upon my other agent," the Queen said, "I would appreciate his return as well, if he still lives."

"If he..." Megan looked back at the Queen again. "So, this isn't as easy as it sounds, is it?"

"When the Sword falls out of use, whatever else happens to it, it always hides itself behind challenges, to make sure its next wielder is worthy of it. Findias is the closest of the lost cities, but still quite remote, and beyond the Huntsman's plains." She smiled, the expression—and especially those eyes—briefly transfixing Megan entirely. "But I have no doubt that Riocard's daughter is up for the challenge."

Megan tried to draw her gaze away from eyes the color and intensity of a sunrise, but only managed once Orlaith looked away from her to the man standing next to the throne. When the Queen didn't address them again, Megan took it as a dismissal, and was glad for it.

Once they were out of obvious earshot of the Queen and her attendants, Megan took another look around the room, before asking her question. "So this is where my dad has to show up for a waltz or whatever?"

Ashling giggled. "By the standards of Court tradition, the waltz is so newfangled, it's practically in the same category as twerking."

Chapter 11: The Gray Lady

"So what's next?" Megan asked.

"The Unseelie King's tower, in the west wing of the house," Cassia said, pointing in the right direction.

"Right. We were supposed to meet someone else. With lights?"

"The Gray Lady, your dad's seneschal. She runs the Unseelie Court whenever he's gone," Lani said.

"Should we really be going into, you know, the area that's all Unseelie, without the guards and things?" Megan asked.

Cassia snorted. "Speaking as a card-carrying Unseelie, we're far better off going there without the guards than with them."

"Okay, point taken, if not quite what I meant."

"Yes," Lani said. "We need to go there. It's dangerous, but with Cassia and Ashling along, we should be fine. Besides, your Dad's place may be the best spot to sleep, with this crowd. It's getting too late to head out into the wilds now, and we could stand to stock up on supplies, anyway. I've got some, but a few more won't hurt, and we might find something useful."

They got a lot of questioning looks as they left the main section of the castle and moved through the winding halls. Without Ashling guiding them, Megan, at least, was pretty sure she'd have gotten lost a few times over. When they reached the west wing, the decor took on a decidedly darker edge. There were fewer windows, and while the suits of armor remained, most had weapons at the ready, and not all of them were entirely cleaned of what appeared to be bloodstains. The artwork depicted frenzied revels instead of pastoral scenes and witch burnings instead of gatherings around firelight. The paintings of glorious heroes were replaced by a theme of great hunts, where tall figures, one of whom had horns, chased down hapless mortals with hordes of faeries and giant hunting hounds.

Even the ivy changed, trading in its multi-colored flowers for hooked barbs. She quickly learned to be careful about the thorns after brushing one. Despite her barely touching the vine, the barb drew blood from the back of one hand—and she watched while the droplet of blood on the tip of the thorn was absorbed into the vine.

She once again had to be hurried along at times by her companions, particularly Lani, who seemed especially eager to keep moving. They were challenged in the halls for right-of-way once or twice, but between Cassia and the cats, whom she had chosen not to leave outside with the chariot, the other fae always elected to move aside.

They finally reached what Ashling identified as Riocard's chambers. While the door was initially locked, some protective enchantment on them recognized Ashling. The pixie whispered a few words, which a light wind picked up. Megan listened in fascination as the same syllables repeated over and over, muted by a whistling wind in the formerly still hallway, and then the door simply creaked open as the winds stilled.

The leopard without a helmet pushed through the doorway first, followed by his brother. Cassia followed. Megan and Lani exchanged a glance, then followed. Megan paused, noticing Ashling wasn't following. Instead, she remained astride the Count as he settled on top of the open door. "Coming?" Megan finally asked.

"No thanks. He has a thing for perching atop chamber doors, at least for those lacking busts of Pallas. It makes him feel especially literary."

"I hear she didn't really have much of a bust," Cassia commented.

Megan eyed the pair for a few more moments, shrugged, and continued into the room. Riocard's chambers weren't a mess, not precisely. Rather, the chaos and mismatched elements of the room were neatly organized and perhaps designed with strange contrasts in mind. A pair of light, curved swords were mounted on the wall, with a Fender Stratocaster hung up between them. An entire wall of the massive chamber was lined with thick tomes— judging by the lettering, apparently written in dozens of different languages. Amongst all of the weighty books, however, were some more legible oddities, such as worn copies of *The Anarchist's*

Cookbook and *A Clockwork Orange*. When the shelves reached the corner, the bookcase continued, but the expanse of shelves there that covered a third of the wall held the most impressive collection of CDs, cassette tapes, records, and the odd 8-track that Megan had ever seen.

At the center of the room was an open display case, containing a figure, nearly six and a half feet tall, of a dark, thorny material, though there appeared to be some sort of threads of mossy silk in parts. Strange as the armor was, the mask was the most notable. Though no part of the face was left uncovered, there was multiple layers to the twisting thorns there, giving it some depth, and, she imagined, the look as if the face was in the middle of some savage howl of joy. The only real gaps were where the thorn branches parted, just a little, leaving room for the wearer's eyes, though even there, the combination of thorns jutting into the open space and the slant of the gaps made it appear more sinister.

"What's that?" Megan asked.

"Riocard's armor," Cassia explained, strutting over to it. "Mostly only wears it for special occasions. You have no idea how long it takes to weave all the enchantments for good briarmail." She knocked on one of the arm bracers. The sound echoed.

Megan reached over to mimic the knocking and repeat the sound, but as she touched the armor, the thorns started to unwind from the display frame and wrap themselves around her arm.

"Megan!" Lani shouted as the armor warped around, and Cassia quickly grabbed Megan and dragged her back. The thorns paused, then wound themselves back around their frame.

Megan flailed at first, but... "I'm... I'm okay," she said between half-panicked breaths.

"It didn't hurt you?" Lani asked.

"No," Megan looked at her arm, which had not a scratch. "Felt kinda silky, now that I think of it. Just creepy as anything, obviously."

"Yeah."

"Hello," came a soft singsong whisper.

Megan almost worried for a moment that the armor was talking, before the little wisp of light came whirling around in front of her. She recognized the presence of a will o' wisp this time, the little ball soon hovering just inside the doorway. "Hello?"

"The Gray Lady will see you now," came the melodic whisper.

They followed as the will o' wisp retreated from the room and headed to an audience chamber not far away.

The room wasn't as grand as the ballroom, but was still impressive. As the centerpiece of the room, four legs of twisted wood seemed to grow directly out of the stone floors, the ensuing branches entwining to form a meeting table. The chairs were less rooted, but of similar design, though each had velvet-lined backs and cushions. At the head of the table stood a woman in a dark gray cloak. Her only accompaniment was a will o' wisp, soon joined by the one that had guided them, which floated over to hover just to the woman's left.

Her hair looked like layers of silver wire that had been allowed to tarnish. Her eyes were like blank mirrors, expressionless. That there were dark circles under her eyes was too much understatement. There and only there, her skin was jet black, the rest being a sickly pale color. From the corners of her eyes to her jaw, disappearing only under the cloak where it clasped at her throat, rivulets of mother-of-pearl were somehow overlaid or stained on her skin. The streaks shone like eerily trailing rainbow teardrops when the light hit them.

Megan curtsied, following Lani's example, while Cassia bowed deeply. Ashling and the Count settled in at the table, the pixie dismounting from the crow, while looking at the woman distrustfully. The Gray Lady ignored the pixie's lack of respect, head turning slightly as a sign that her blank eyes were passing over each of them in turn, before she appeared to settle on Megan. Her mouth didn't move. The only voice came from the will o' wisps. "The Unseelie King's Daughter. I should have known that those years he was gone so often, our King was pursuing his fascination with mortals."

Megan paused, a little unsure whether to address the woman or the glowing ball of light. She finally managed, "Yes, that's me," before growing a little bolder. "And I'm here to find my father."

"Of course you are," the will o' wisps said, "But you're running out of time."

"I know. Less than two weeks until Halloween. You're his seneschal. Do you know anything that would help us? Or maybe you could help out? While he's gone, the Unseelie listen to you, right?"

The Gray Lady's lip turned upward for a brief moment. Megan took it as a sign of her finding something terribly amusing. "The Unseelie have at least mostly obeyed my edict to stay out of the mountains and the Winter Marches."

"Stay out of them? But that's where my dad disappeared. With enough people, surely you'd be able to find him."

"Or lose more people to the same trap or treachery."

"Sorry to put it like this, but it doesn't sound like you've done a lot to find my dad, if you're keeping people away from where he disappeared."

"I have done what I found necessary to secure the people under our responsibility. Orlaith, apparently—" the Gray Lady frowned slightly, "—has a plan."

"Yeah. We're going to get the Sword of Light and go cut my dad out of whatever's got him."

"That may work," came the whispers. "A last resort. But we should consider this thoroughly. Possibly send someone older and more experienced."

Megan straightened herself as much as possible, looking up at her. "Well, looks like you're running out of time, and I'm the only half-human you've got lying around who can get the sword, so I'll get back to you about precautions when I have it."

The haunted, iridescent eyes in the gaunt, iridescent-mottled face stared for a moment. "Very well. Good luck." The Gray Lady bowed her head, turned, and walked away, trailed by the pale balls of light.

Chapter 12: Dining-Room Blitz

Despite Cassia's assurances, Megan and Lani alike insisted they didn't want to remain in the west wing for dinner. Ashling, after checking that Riocard's door was locked, led them through the twists and turns toward the more shared areas of the castle. A glance into one of the dining halls along the way made Megan all the happier for her choice. While the food was largely identifiable, and at least not human, the sight of some of the creatures within tearing their food apart, snapping bones to get at the marrow, or consuming whole organs pulled from the carcasses almost made Megan lose her appetite.

The scent of food coming from one of the larger halls brought most of it back.

"Yeah," she said. "This is far enough. I'm starving."

Entering, they were met immediately by what Megan was pretty sure was a brownie, judging by her previous encounters. The short, rumpled person led them to seats near the head of the table, then curtsied and scampered off. Before long, another one that Megan was pretty sure was a bit more masculine brought them drinks. Megan was about to drink when Lani put her hand on the cup.

"Megan will have a glass of water," she whispered to the brownie—as much as it could be a whisper in a crowded room. "And so will I." He nodded and shuffled off again.

Cassia and Ashling hadn't seemed to notice, the former draining her own cup and demanding another, while Ashling and the Count worked out sharing a cup, ignoring the offer of something more suitably pixie-sized.

Megan looked at Lani expectantly. "Faerie food and drink, especially drink, can be tricky stuff," Lani muttered. "To be safest, avoid the fruits and the wine."

Megan nodded her understanding. Water glasses followed, and the food was served not long after.

Megan did her best to keep Lani's warning in mind, though her mind kept wandering off through the meal. There were several occasions where her hand almost reached for a huge, juicy golden raspberry from the bowl on the table before her eyes met a worried menehune frown. Still, she wasn't deprived. The rest of the food was the best she could recall having ever eaten, with flavors that were somehow fuller and richer than she could remember tasting, in the same way the colors were brighter, and the mountains taller. Of course, it helped not to have any appetite-suppressing medication anymore, too.

The table brought a constant show to go with the meal as well, with what seemed to Megan to be at least half a dozen different languages being spoken around her, by all manner of faerie creatures. She kept trying to make mental notes about the look of the laden bowls of multicolored fruit, or of the bunny-person, or the twisted-faced goblin next to him, or of the guy in black who ... set his head down on the table while he cut his steak. She wanted to memorize each sight to draw later, but always found her eyes wandering on to the next oddity.

Her attention was drawn back to her immediate surroundings when she heard Cassia exchanging heated words in a language she didn't understand with what she guessed was a leprechaun, based on stature and dress. As they spoke, more and more of the faeries at the table started to rise to bunch around one or the other, showing their support, but starting to make Megan feel rather crowded. She looked to Lani, and the pair started looking for a way out of the crowd, but didn't see any easy gaps as more and more people were rising from their spots at the table to gather around.

The tension broke when the leprechaun splashed the contents of his mug at Cassia. The easy smile Megan had gotten used to on the satyr's face twisted into an animalistic snarl, and Cassia lunged, leaping to the table top in the process. When the smaller faerie dodged, she ended up tackling one of the hag things instead, sending her flying into one of the knots of redcaps and less identifiable but unsavory-looking things. From there, there was no stopping the brawl.

Megan grabbed for Lani's hand, holding tight. Lani pulled suddenly, dragging Megan out of the way of a staggering thing with a goat's head. Megan returned the favor by dragging Lani to the floor before they were struck with a flying chair. The guy in black hadn't even put his head back on before getting involved.

In the process of standing back up, she came eye-to-eye with one of the brownies. "King's daughter, this way," the small girl—at least she thought this one was a girl—said. Megan at first wondered how she knew, but supposed word would get around all the faster after her father had enforced his secret for so long. Still clutching Lani's hand, she did her best to weave through the crowd after the brownie, who seemed to know precisely the right places to dodge in navigation of the shifting melee.

When they reached the far wall, the brownie gestured, then backed against the wall. Megan only realized what happened when she looked to either side of herself. Lani and the brownie, and Megan herself, she supposed, blended into the wall perfectly. She watched the fight going back and forth for some time, eyes darting around the room, and otherwise trying to stay very still lest the brownie's illusion fail.

Things were starting to settle again, as if on some kind of cue she couldn't detect, when she noticed him. The '49ers redcap was sitting at the far end of the table, stripping the meat off a chicken bone with those jagged, graying teeth, paying the fight no mind. Even with people moving between them, his gaze never wavered— illusion or not, he was looking towards Megan and just smiling while he ate.

When things did settle enough that the brownie dropped the illusion, the girls were only too happy to leave, even when offered more food and drink. A slightly weaving Ashling and a grinning Cassia, now with a brand new black eye, chose to follow along, heading back for Riocard's room. The redcap stayed at the table but continued to follow Megan with his gaze until she'd rounded the corner.

Chapter 13: A Semi-Restless Night

Megan stayed away from the armor this time as they went to bed down. She kept looking around. There were a few pictures amid everything else on the walls. Most were masterworks that echoed the themes of the paintings decorating the halls, but one especially stood out, mostly for its stark contrast. At the edge of a wooded area, a redheaded woman in ancient, rustic garb had dropped to one knee. One of her hands rested on the head of a calf, standing calmly next to her. The other hand was outstretched towards a tree, with a green snake winding its way out of the tree and around her arm. The woman had a serene expression, but her bright green eyes were intense, painted so lifelike that Megan swore they followed her.

"Who's that?" she asked, even as the thought hit her that the features reminded her a little of old photos of her mother—only the oldest ones, with her hair literally and figuratively down. Megan had never known her mother to have as much life in her as the painting did.

"The Goddess Brigid," Cassia said, as she took the blankets folded to set herself up on the floor while Lani and Megan shared the bed. "When Riocard was young, he knew her son."

"Oh. Huh. Bridget is my middle name," Megan remarked.

"Of course it is," Cassia said.

Megan shrugged, then canted her head slightly. "I've heard the Gods mentioned a couple of times. So, if faeries are real, I'm guessing some of them are, too?"

"Are, were, something like that," Cassia said. "But Brigid and all the rest left, as part of sealing the Fomoire away. They set a lot of things in motion, then left the fae to keep an eye on things. At least these Gods. There's different stories, and different enemies. Only a few, like Riocard, Orlaith, her General Inwar, and the Gray Lady, actually remember a time when the Gods were still around. But it's worked. The Fomoire, the Titans, all of the Giants—they're all gone too."

Lani glanced at Cassia like there was something more to the story, but the satyr shrugged as she arranged the blankets and folded a few maps. Lani sighed, looking to Megan. "We'll talk about it more later. Let's just check for anything worth packing for a trip into the wilderness, then get to bed."

Megan agreed, and resumed looking around, less interested in sleep than in learning about her father. In her wanderings, her eyes settled on an antique grand piano, shoved casually out of the way and left to gather dust. What wasn't dusty, however, was one of the books of music resting on it. Megan quickly determined that she had no idea what the actual wording said, but she could read the notes. As she did, she began to hear an odd melody in her head, unlike any song she'd ever heard, and after a short while of imagining the sound, an image flashed through her brain of gusts of wind carrying Autumn leaves along. She closed her eyes, allowing herself to continue hearing the notes in her mind, and the Autumn imagery became more prominent. She only stopped when she felt Lani's hand on her shoulder, shaking her gently. "What?"

"You were humming, and, well, you probably shouldn't," Lani said, gesturing to the floor. Stacks of loose paper from the piano's song selections littered the floor, and a few more sheets were still lazily drifting downward.

"I did that?" Megan asked, eyes following one of the sheets down.

"You are half-sidhe. You were bound to run into some sort of magic sometime."

"Huh," Megan began, fighting off the temptation to begin humming the tune again. "I wonder what sort of magic Lindsay Stirling covers would do."

"Can we not find out just now?" Lani asked. "I'd like to sleep. Tomorrow's going to be a long, long day."

"Sure, fair enough." Megan agreed, getting into the bed, but only after picking up the papers and putting the music book with the packed things.

"Personally," Cassia contributed from the floor, "I think punk violinists make a kind of a magic you need to find out about when you're older."

Megan tried to bed down. "These are nice pillows at least," she said.

"Quality pillows are very important to royalty," Ashling said. "Not to mention the importance of under-pillow storage and commerce."

"...What, like the Tooth Fairy?"

"My cousin Nessa used to do Tooth Fairy work, a long, long time ago. Her unit was reassigned due to their real creative solution to not having exact change."

Megan just sighed and didn't ask any further.

Getting to sleep wasn't easy. The looming risk, combined with trying to absorb that everything around her was real, and was really happening, kept Megan awake. Somewhere amidst tossing and turning and pondering how easily Cassia and Ashling drifted off even with tomorrow's adventure ahead of them, Megan finally managed.

In her dreams, she saw herself standing on a carpet of fallen leaves, with the book of music in hand. She started turning the pages, sight-reading the music, singing words she didn't understand. As she did, the wind gradually rose around her, picking up the leaves and carrying them along. The leaves swirled around Megan, lifting and spinning and dancing to the tune. Gradually, both melody and words changed, shifting from the unknown music to the sounds of "Radioactive."

As it did, she heard a saxophone managing to accompany it. Turning with the swirl of wind, she saw Cassia, playing her sax in time with the winds. Strings joined in, as the satyr's dreadlocked violinist girlfriend stepped up beside her. More joined, and Megan spun around the other way. The woman playing the bass guitar was her mother, but as she played, her hair came loose from the severe bun, and she shook the long red locks free. The woman's business jacket seemed almost to slough away or disintegrate, revealing her rock band t-shirt, as her attention never wavered from her bassline.

Somewhere in the midst of her playing, a green snake starting winding down her arm.

The music abruptly changed, a version of the "Game of Thrones" theme now. The whirling leaves sped up, and Cassia and Megan's mother switched songs and tempo without missing a beat, as the lead guitar line echoed on the wind, originating somewhere behind Megan. As she started to turn, she woke up—everyone else was still sleeping, and the room was dark. Still, she knew the pages of music were scattered around her again, and even in the dark, she could see Brigid's intense green eyes staring at her.

Chapter 14: Venturing into the Wilds

"So which way are we headed?" Megan asked as Cassia hitched up the cats and put the extra pack of supplies in the chariot.

"That way," Ashling indicated. "Towards the Unfordable River."

"Sounds reassuring," Megan said dryly.

"Don't worry," Ashling said, "We're headed for the part with the flesh-eating fish, not any of the Jenny Greenteeths, Greentooths, Jennies Greenteeth ... well, there's a bunch of them. Twenty-seven, I think. They might have gone to school together."

Megan sighed. "Flesh-eating fish?"

"And fast-moving rapids. And we're right between a couple of the whirlpools. They'll occasionally try to meander out a bit, just to see if they can get in on the drowning-people action," Ashling said.

"Whirlpools... don't usually do that."

"Not the whirlpools you're used to," Lani said, "Keep in mind where you're at. The environment is going to have a certain attitude about things sometimes."

"And we do not just mean flora and fauna," Ashling said in an attempt to re-seize the conversation. "The magic in the very essence of a place will care deeply about some things and not others. The ballroom at An Teach Deiridh has an incredibly hidebound, aristocratic personality, and there's no reasoning with it—although my cousin Nessa tried once. With visual aids."

Lani continued the original subject. "Besides, the river has to be pretty bad in order to keep the pack on the other side."

"Pack?" Megan asked, not liking the sound of this.

"You saw some of the pictures of the Wild Hunt. When the huntsman calls them, they can come to him over anything, to anywhere. The rest of the time, when they're not chasing someone down, they need somewhere to be. The plains on the other side of the river is it."

"Oh, well of course. So we're crossing an uncrossable river, in order to go hang out with some hounds that love nothing better than running people down?"

"That's only when the huntsman calls them," Cassia said, "Without his magic behind them, sometimes they like to chase, sometimes they just like to sunbathe. And they're not quite as tireless, only mostly."

"Still, very reassuring," Megan responded.

"Megan, we're going to manage it," Lani said, catching up and laying a hand on Megan's shoulder, "I have some ideas."

"Besides," said Ashling, "Getting there is just half the challenge. Findias itself is bound to be much worse. Enough people have gone there and back that we know about the rivers and hounds. No one gets past the front gates, or if they do, they haven't come back."

"Are you sure you're Seelie?" Megan asked the overly cheerful pixie.

"You get too hung up on the teams things," Ashling answered. "Seelie just comes from an old word meaning cheerful anyway."

"I thought you said it was punctual."

"Punctuality is among my virtues, but it's definitely all about the cheerful part."

"What about the Queen and her General, and those knights? They looked pretty serious."

"On the outside, sure. Inside, they're singing show tunes and doing high kicks. Trust me."

Megan blinked, trying to picture that and failing. "If you say so. Are you going to tell me the real story of where faeries come from next?"

Lani grinned at Megan, "You're catching on," she said quietly.

"Of course I am," Ashling responded without taking any notice of sarcasm or Lani's response, "Faeries come from the dust the eldest Gods rubbed out of their eyes when they first awoke."

"Fascinating," Megan said, "Now, just to check, if Seelie means cheerful, does that mean Unseelie means not cheerful? Because the Gray Lady kind of looks it, but Cassia..."

"I'm crying on the inside," Cassia said without missing a beat.

"I'm sure you are," Megan said.

"You'd think so, but they're actually totally unrelated words, very different entomologies," Ashling said.

"I think you mean etymologies," Megan replied.

"I would, except Unseelie are descended from dragonflies, so it totally applies."

"Aren't Unseelie still faeries?"

"Well of course they are. Are you still worried about the teams thing? There's not as much difference as you seem to think. Sure, the Unseelie are more prone to, say, eat people or cheer for the villain in slasher flicks, but otherwise, not so different."

Megan was about to respond, but Lani shook her head. "I'll keep that in mind," Megan replied instead of her previous question. She reviewed the conversation in her head. "Speaking of the Gray Lady, if will o' wisps feed on emotion, why're some hanging out with her? She's got more of a zombie thing going than an emotional thing."

"Grief is an emotion," Cassia said. "Those wisps just don't mind getting the same thick, juicy steak five meals a day."

"What happened?"

"She lost her kid. A long, long time ago, but it kind of overwhelmed her identity. She's not a zombie. She's a bean sidhe."

"Banshee? I thought they screamed. She doesn't even talk."

"Let's just be glad of that, okay?"

After walking a little further in relative quiet, Megan finally asked the other question that had been bothering her. "So, that redcap, the one who chased us before, and was hanging out with his buddies back at—"

"An Teach Deiridh," Lani filled in.

"Yeah, that place," Megan said. "How likely is it he's going to get a bunch of his buddies and come after us now? I mean, obviously someone trapped my father, and they won't want us to get the sword."

"About even odds," Cassia said, "Depending on how much they really want to stop you versus how much they don't want to upset the Queen, or be on Riocard's bad side if you succeed."

"But they came after me before."

"Sure, but no one cared then. You were on Earth. A few of us like the place, but most faeries only visit every now and then. Now, lots of people are watching. You're not just some mortal who doesn't know anything, anymore. You're the King's daughter. People will notice, and care, if you disappear now."

"But they might still come after us?"

"Oh sure. They could. Obviously, someone put an awful lot of effort and magical resources into this. Trapping Riocard isn't a small feat. You don't live for thousands of years, and rule for a lot of those, by being an idiot."

"You don't seem very worried."

"If they come after us, we'll deal with it. I think they're much more likely to hope the river, the hounds, or the city kill us. Of course, I could be wrong."

"And if you are?"

"Then I figure out which of the cats to listen to."

"Which of the cats?"

"Well, yes. Maxwell is pretty sure we can outfight a gang of redcaps or hags or bogies or whatever else there is."

"And Jude?"

Cassia grinned in a way that didn't suggest she wasn't being entirely serious. "He's pretty sure we can outrun you."

Chapter 15: The Unfordable River

The girls looked over the roiling water.

"Well.... Cassia... can you possibly jump it in that thing, if you got enough of a start?"

Cassia surveyed the river. "...Nope," she said at last.

Meanwhile, the leopard on the left was intently focused ahead, muscles tensing under his fur.

"Maxwell really wants to try, though," Cassia added.

For a while, they all sat in the near-tangible moonlight, which suffused the night air the way the golden haze had the day. The girls munched on the granola bars and sandwiches that Lani had packed for reasons of Lani. Megan was starving. Of course, she'd been constantly hungry ever since the orange pills hadn't been orange pills anymore. Of course, for this trip, she hadn't even brought the multi-colored ones.

After this makeshift supper, Lani sighed. "Okay, Blankets out. Everyone needs to go to sleep."

"What?" Megan asked. "You think the situation'll get better if we sleep on it?"

"Sort of," said Lani. "Not in the biological equivalent of tech support way—" at the raised eyebrows, Lani sighed again at having to explain her joke. "The 'have you tried turning it off, and then on again' way. Anyway, never mind. I just need everybody to sleep, and then I'll handle it. But you have to be asleep."

"What, are you Santa Claus now?"

"Wrong kind of jolly old elf. Or elf-like thing. Look, there are Restrictions, okay? What I need to do is a night-time thing, a non-menehune-are-asleep thing."

It was Megan's turn to sigh. "Fine, fine. Just....watch out for owls."

"Just go to sleep."

They made a makeshift camp, once Cassia agreed her chariot wouldn't be too harmed by a little industrial use. So Megan curled up in the blankets and lay back. The stars burned bright high above, with an intensity, and a feeling of nearness Megan never remembered stars possessing before. She'd heard in freshman science class that the hotter stars burned, the more fuel they were using up. Recalling that, she'd swear half the stars in the sky could disappear at any moment.

She closed her eyes, trying to ignore the sounds of moving wheels and sliding objects, which became strangely fast as she drifted.

Megan dreamed of the castle hallways.

One of the people she'd seen about the prescriptions her mother wanted had told Megan that dreams weren't accessible to all five senses. The scent of some kind of barbecue wafted through the halls nevertheless. Megan followed her nose, ravenous, around twist after twist and turn after turn in the bizarre complex of ornate carpets, stained wood, and bare stone. She waved to a passing bloodthirsty vine. When she came upon the dining hall the smell was coming from, a sea of nightmare faces crowded around a long table, leaving only one chair empty. The huge bird dressed in the middle as the main course was not a roasted, seasoned chicken or turkey or even something like a duck or goose. It had three heads.

Megan stood in the doorway staring at this for a while, but she was still hungry. A large figure with rough hands the size of her head passed her a fork. She took the empty seat. As bones—both those on the plates and those within the arms of some shoving, elbowing diners—cracked open across the table, Megan had her meal.

When she woke, all she could think was that it was delicious.

She wasn't thinking about whether she was supposed to get up, in the not-quite-light of not-quite-dawn.

"Megan!" Lani shouted, suddenly grabbing onto the riverbank.

Megan looked around. A collection of small trees had been uprooted. Their stumps stood on the riverbank, sliced into angled wedges of varying heights, a different rope tied around each. Across the river, the higher ropes provided handholds as the lower ones were bound together with logs for stepping. The logs started off extremely close but eventually became much sparser. On the opposite side of the riverbank, the sets of ropes were held down by—or attached to—several large rocks.

"Ah. Not done. Right. Sorry, I'll try to go back to sleep."

"Nope. Doesn't work," Lani said, pulling herself up. "You made it count as morning. This job is over."

"Sorry. Oh, well. We'll just be really, really careful for the last bit." Megan looked over as the others were getting up ... and looked at the chariot. "... oh, yeah."

Cassia stepped over and kicked one of the wedge-stumps, finding that it had, apparently, taken root again. She gauged the level of the slant of the combined area of wood. She and Lani exchanged grins for a moment, then the satyress looked back. "What do you think, boys?"

The leopard in the aviator helmet sniffed hesitantly. His brother simply stood himself near the chariot, muscles tensing again.

Cassia hitched her cats up and took the chariot far back, to where cleared trees had previously been. After a few moments, Jude and Maxwell started running.

In sophomore biology, Megan had learned that the peregrine falcon is the fastest living animal. For a moment, watching the big cats build up speed, it was harder to believe. As they ran up the rickety-but-rooted ramp, the leopards roared like, well, a motorcycle engine. Above that was simply a high-pitched "Yeeeeee-haa!"

Both girls let out a breath Megan didn't know they were holding when the wheels of the chariot hit the opposite bank by the slightest margin. Various bits of grass and chips of bark kicked up into the water by the jump attracted the attention of strange, large fish with noticeable teeth.

"Well, our turn now," Lani said. She looked at the water. "A bit ...uhm ... slower, and more careful."

"Yeah," said Megan.

They tentatively edged their way across the bridge, clutching the ropes more and more as they progressed and had to take wider steps onto fewer logs. As they drew closer to the somewhat less-elaborate moorings on the other side, the ropes drastically angled lower, which meant having to crouch lower to hold on, making it even harder to avoid looking closely at the fish-things that snapped just below the logs. It also made the increasingly bigger steps more awkward.

"Ech. I should have worn gloves," Megan said as her hand and arm were brush-burned by the rope mid-lunge.

"You should have stayed the heck asleep," Lani muttered.

Eventually, they managed to toss themselves on the riverbank, breathing heavily for a moment, while Cassia, Ashling, Jude, and the Count all stared at them. Maxwell was busy staring at the snapping fish-things, though Cassia said, "Maxwell, no," without even looking at him.

Cassia then took some of the scattered logs Lani's frenetic menehune activity had left on that side of the river and started to bind them together with rope from the chariot's pack. Lani occasionally glanced over as she was drawing herself up, twitched slightly, and muttered under her breath about workmanship and Restrictions.

"No rules for me, kiddo," Cassia said cheerfully as she propped the improvised ramp against the stones. "There. That'll be something for the way back."

"Is this really the time to be planning the way back?" Megan asked.

"You think we'll have time when we've just stolen a magic sword?"

Chapter 16: The Hounds

Now that she could stop worrying about falling into the river, Megan's attention shifted to worrying about the hounds. She was certain that with all the noise Cassia had made, the smell of the cats, the smell of people, or just bad luck, there would be snarling monster hounds investigating at any moment.

Despite her nightmare imaginings, the area remained quiet. Unfortunately, with the terrain shifting from the plains and wooded terrain on the other side of the river to rocky hills, she also had little idea how big the area was, or how close any of the hounds might be. Suspecting the baying monsters from the paintings around any turn or just behind every rise was, to her mind, almost as bad as actually seeing them. Given the slow and careful progress of the group, Ashling's general quiet, and even Cassia and the cats' going tense, Megan guessed she wasn't alone in her paranoia.

She continued to trust in Ashling's sense of direction, the crow flying out over the hills and scouting ahead, then wheeling back to be certain the others were still following. Despite the extra effort in scaling the occasionally difficult hills, particularly for the chariot, the small group kept making the effort, pausing at the top of each rise to look around at the territory below. Megan always felt safest on the hilltops, but, of course, they couldn't stay there for long.

With the group in the midst of one of the climbs down the back side of one large hill, Ashling and the Count came diving back to the group. "They'recomingthey'recomingrunrunnow!" the pixie shouted all the way. At least she did right up until the point where a nightmare beast came racing over the top of a hill, leaping without hesitation, trying to snap at the bird in mid-air. Either Ashling or the crow noticed in time, and managed to climb, but the Count still lost a couple of tail feathers.

Megan stopped, mid-climb, just staring at the monster dog. She was pretty sure she'd seen a few horses that weren't quite that big—and it sounded like it was just the first of many. Sounds of baying started echoing through the hills.

"Megan, come on!" Lani shouted, tugging at Megan's jacket. The pair began to run, almost stumbling a few times. Cassia finally reached back, pulling each of them onto the chariot, though they had to split their effort between clutching the side of the chariot and clinging to Cassia to stay in place, as the satyr urged the leopards into a full run. The vehicle bounced and rattled down the hill. More than once, Megan was pretty sure it was going to flip over—at least as many times as she felt like she was going to be thrown free despite her death-grip, and almost as many as the times she thought she was about to be sick.

They reached the bottom in one piece, and Cassia turned sharply, trying to stay in the valleys between the hills so she wouldn't lose speed. Megan, glancing back, started catching sight of more and more massive forms emerging from all over the area, scaling hills to get a view of the area, and forming up into packs before tearing after them.

Caught up in watching the horde forming up behind them, Megan's head whirled around when she heard one of the cats howl a warning, followed by cursing from Cassia in what Megan was pretty sure was at least three languages. She'd heard of packs of dogs or wolves working together to drive prey into traps, which was what she was guessing had just happened, as more of the monster beasts were swarming out over the nearby hilltops.

Cassia pulled on a rein, and the cats turned sharply, taking the chariot up an incline and over rocky outcroppings large enough to briefly send the vehicle into the air, landing awkwardly on one wheel. Cassia leaned hard the other direction, and despite spending a few moments tipped precariously, the chariot came down on both wheels—just in time for Cassia to need to turn sharply again. She barely avoided the closest hound as it leaped from the top of the hill they'd been climbing, landing where they'd have been had Cassia's reflexes been any less.

"Thiswaythisway!" Ashling called frantically from nearby. Without hesitation, Cassia turned the chariot and charged in the direction of the pixie's voice. Despite the risk of low altitude, the Count dropped to just ahead of the leopards, leading the way at high speed. More of the hounds were closing in on either side of them, but they stayed just ahead of the packs, though a few snapping jaws got close enough that Megan could feel the hot breath.

"Ashling! Higher!" Megan heard herself calling, more than a little surprised that her first thoughts were of getting at least the pixie out of reach. She was even more surprised when the flighty little creature looked back, shook her head firmly, and continued to lead the way, rising only to make sure they were still on a clear path, making adjustments for Cassia to follow.

The chariot made another jump, landing amidst stones and dirt loose enough to send it skidding off to one side, briefly pulling one of the leopards off balance. The shift in momentum was enough to break Lani's grip, and she went tumbling over the side of the chariot, landing hard and headfirst. The cats recovered enough to take off at a run again, either not noticing or not caring that they'd left a passenger behind.

"Lani!" Megan called, leaping off the back of the chariot, reaching her friend before the nearest hounds did. With Lani trying to struggle to her feet, obviously dizzy, Megan tackled her out of the way of the nearest hound.

With more hounds coming from seemingly all directions, Megan did the first thing that came to mind—singing a few bars of the first song she thought of at the top of her lungs. To her surprise, a sudden gust of intense wind picked up some of the loose dirt and debris, carrying it into the eyes of the frontmost hounds.

The lead dogs pulled up short, trying to shake the irritants out of their eyes, and the hounds behind them crashed into the lead rank. Megan tried again, hitting the next bars as another hound came at them. This time, nothing happened. She tensed, seeing the creature bearing down on her, before it pulled up short, snapping at a black, feathered form that just clawed at the side of his head.

"Megan, go!" Ashling shouted, dive bombing a few more of the hounds, weaving and climbing and turning the small pack around.

Once Megan helped Lani to her feet, the two started to run again, though unlike last time they went at a full sprint, now it was Lani who was lagging behind, visibly almost losing her balance a few times. Megan slowed. Lani opened her mouth as if to argue, but Megan interrupted. "Not leaving you."

Coming around another hill, Megan saw a flat expanse, extending quite some way, before reaching another rise, this one an almost vertical wall of rocks and occasional grass patches. From here, it looked like a trap, somewhere the hounds would pin them against with nowhere to run, provided they didn't just run them down in the open plain, which seemed far more likely.

Then her eyes settled on Cassia and the cats, turned and waiting for them. Megan tugged on Lani's arm, starting towards the satyr even as the baying picked up again. A glance back confirmed that the distraction was over, and the hounds were in pursuit again. She turned her head back around, starting to sprint for Cassia, who appeared to be talking to someone—and the cats, though looking agitated, were howling and hissing back. Cassia finally seemed to reach a consensus, shaking her head at the girls running her way.

Just as Megan was thinking she was about to abandon them, Cassia instead pointed towards the vertical rise in the distance. Megan gave another panicked glance back, then looked at Cassia again. The satyr gestured again, more insistent, and Megan altered her course, just sprinting for the wall.

A howl unlike anything Megan had ever heard drew her gaze again. She'd seen the expression, or something like it, on Cassia's face before, when the leprechaun had splashed her. Now, it was even more intense, the woman's face flushing darker as she shouted. Both cats joined in the howl, and the chariot took off again—but this time towards the pack of hounds. The war cry and battle howl began to turn into a grin—but it was somehow no less savage, as the chariot rocketed forward, with Cassia calling "Euan

Euan Eu-Oi-Oi-Oi!" as they charged. The unexpected tactic took the hounds off guard, and at first, they parted before her berserk rush.

Once Cassia had their attention, more of the hounds turning her way, the chariot spun around and raced off, with the surprised dogs gathering up and taking off in pursuit again. It was only when she heard Ashling's shouts again that Megan turned back around, moving faster once she stopped watching the high speed chase. Lani was picking up speed, along with better balance, with the recovery time, and Ashling kept looping back around to make sure both girls were focused ahead and ignoring the shouts and howls and baying behind them.

It seemed to take forever, and both girls were thoroughly out of breath as they finally reached the wall. Megan craned her neck upward, looking at the sheer wall ahead of them. "That's... a long way up."

Chapter 17: Reunion of a Sort

"Lani?" Megan asked with a strain in her voice as she hauled herself up.

"Yeah?"

"Just realized something." A deep breath as she reached for the next handhold, then exhaling. "I'm a Faerie Princess."

"Legally, yeah." Lani scrambled ahead of her again.

"When do I get my gosh-darn wings and tiara?"

"If you do," Ashling said quietly, "watch out for butterfly collectors."

That got things silent for a minute, as the two girls dragged themselves onto the grass and got out the snacks from Lani's pack. For once, Ashling didn't seem eager to tell a story.

In the silence came a sound on the wind. "Megan." It was a whisper at first, then louder. "Megan can you hear me?" asked the voice like chocolate.

"Whoa," Lani said.

"I... yeah..." Megan muttered. "Dad?" She immediately wished she had managed to make her first conscious words to her father something a bit more impressive.

"Good to hear from you, Sir," Ashling said.

"And you as well. Ashling, Lani Kahale, Counts-to-18. Could you excuse the two of us for a few minutes?"

"Of course." And the crow rose into the air and flew a little way farther, Lani following.

"So you can talk, even though you're frozen or whatever out there?"

"My dear, Winter is My Time. The ice might be around me, but it's not going to subdue me. It's only because of a terribly clever use of wards and location that I'm stuck at all, and enough effort and preparation can get the occasional communication out. The real salt in the wound is, well, the salt."

"I'm guessing the salt is another faerie issue I don't know about. Lani knows about the Menehune-Brownie Strategic Alliance of 1801. I'm still not sure what 'Seelie' means."

"Yes," the voice on the wind replied. "But you're managing wonderfully, no doubt."

"Her dad probably explained a lot of stuff."

"I'm quite certain he did. Parenting seems to be the sole menehune job which mustn't be done in one night."

Megan sat and thought for a moment, then took a breath. "You left when I was two."

"Yes. Two years, two months, two days, and I'll swear on your middle name that it wasn't that you were less than delightful," the voice said with quiet warmth on the cool breeze. "I stopped back home for the Dance, found out there was a full-blown political crisis, and couldn't foist off the responsibilities anymore."

"Why didn't you come back?"

"Well, I was very busy, and by the time you were in kindergarten, your mother was very cross."

Well, there was no arguing with that. Cross was one of her mom's defining characteristics, along with tired. Megan had seen a lifetime of cross and tired. She remembered Cassia's words, though.

"There's more to it than that, though, isn't there?"

"There's always more to it, Megan. One realizes one has said 'just one more day' a few hundred times too many." The wind shifted, and she could almost feel a shrug and a smile. "So your friends are trying to help."

"Yeah...mostly because the Dance is supposed to be important. Lani thinks it's like climate change or something."

There was a silence in the wind, but not the absent kind of silence. It was the silence of people thinking as they sit next to each other. Then, the chocolatey voice spoke. "From a passing acquaintance with her father, that seems reasonable."

"You'd think she'd be allergic to all the science stuff. Isn't that sort of the opposition? Like vampires and churches."

A chuckle in the wind. "Not at all. Science itself is no particular bane. For that matter, neither are churches. I love science.

I love religion. I love how they create wonder and stories and open up minds. I love that they open up the big 'whys.' The only time they're a problem is when people stop wondering, stop grasping for those whys. When the thought that an unseen hand, or some invisible set of rules, drives things makes people search for the answers and meaning, or striving to get closer to those things—that's marvelous. It's only when people stop wondering, stop searching, stop researching, or stop caring about the whys, and just have a pat answer of 'Because science,' or 'Because God,' before they move on—that's when those things become anathema to faeries."

"Oh." Megan took a moment to process that. Her dad apparently had a thing for rhetoric, but then, he was in politics, even if it was faerie politics. Suddenly she asked, "Counts-to-18?"

"The best translation anyone can manage of the Corvid deed-name. It's for his cleverness: most crows only count to 16."

"Oh." She paused. "We may have left Cassia to be eaten by dogs," Megan confessed.

"The hounds deserve their legend, but I suspect that's not how her story ends. I've known her for most of her life. I don't recall her being left to be anything for quite some time, so I suspect she had a hand in the matter."

"It was her idea, yeah."

"Then all's well. Because no matter what your guide and mine says—and this is an important secret—the true distinction of the Unseelie is beyond all good, evil, avarice, passion, ambition, jealousy, and so many other things. It's not that, as the Seelie value order, we value chaos. It's that any Unseelie will always desire at least the option to make the wrong choice."

"Oh." That actually made some sense. Maybe too much sense. "So do you know who did this?"

"Know who ambushed me into this trap? I know several of them, but they did not act on their own initiative. Distinctly not Idea People."

"What happens to them, when you get out?" Megan's mind rushed at all the horrific possibilities, having seen what sort of people her father was technically king of.

"Oh, mostly they'll owe me a favor."

"That's it? After trapping you and risking the climate shift thing, just owing you one?"

"There is no 'Just,' my dear. While it's not a cold iron wound, owing is one of the worst things that can happen to a faerie. Someone else gets the choice. Promises and debts are as real a thing for us as the breath in your lungs and the color of your eyes."

"Okay, then. So anyway, sounds like you can't really tell us who else might try something. We're trying to get the...Cleeves Sole-ish. The Light-Sword."

"The Claiomh Solais. Yes, that figures, considering where you are. I don't know if I'd be able to find you again, without a real energy source against... this. The Claiomh Solais. Well, that's one way of going about it."

"What were you thinking?"

"Well, Mega—" and half the dark whisper was lost on the wind. Then there was something about "hesitate" and "step," again with half the words lost.

"Dad? Dad!"

Then there was something about "losing," "dear," and "good-bye," and then there air was still.

Megan walked in the silence to where Lani was sitting and recovering. Lani opened her mouth, looked at Megan, pulled herself to her feet, and hugged her.

Chapter 18: To the Gates

There was still no sign of Cassia or the cats as the girls made their way to the city. Lani made them stop at a stream, this one thankfully devoid of flesh-eating fish, to refill their canteens. Megan quickly learned why. The terrain rapidly grew more and more lifeless, the green and moss disappearing by the time they went over the last hill.

Finally, she reached the top and caught her first glimpse of the city of Findias. From the distance, it actually looked inviting, at least compared to the hills. The higher buildings, what she could see of them above a dark wall, looked to have once been brightly painted and still bore faded hints of the swirl of colors.

"So, this is one of the lost cities?" Megan asked as they sat to rest.

"It is," Lani said. "There's four of them. Mostly I hear about them as the ultimate remodeling projects. Dad wants to get a huge crew together from the islands and just go to work."

"What happened, anyway?"

Lani looked around to make sure Ashling was out of earshot, but the pixie and crow were safely off in the distance, scouting the route ahead. "Different things to each city. Findias used to be one of the favorites of the fae. It was pretty close to An Teach Deiridh, and the sorcerer who ruled there, Uiscias, used bardic magic, the music stuff. Some of the stories suggest he either taught that type of magic to the Gods, or to their mortal children. I don't know, exactly. Anyway, it used to be a city of music and parties and things."

"I can see why it would be pretty popular. It looks like it was pretty colorful too. And it's not even that ruined. How long has it been abandoned?"

"A really, really long time. The Fomoire drove the faeries out of it. It was one of their last victories before the Gods dragged them off for good. But before they left, they made sure the city would stay mostly standing, but the fae couldn't use it."

"Why not?"

"Cold iron. The whole city is surrounded by it. Everything is locked up. I can't imagine how much work it had to have been, but it was apparently worth it to have the ultimate insult sitting so close."

"My dad mentioned cold iron. I'd even heard of how it's supposed to be bad for faeries. But it's really that nasty, even just as, like, gates?"

"Aside from just the fact injuries from it don't just disappear the way they usually do for a lot of faeries, it cancels their magic."

"That doesn't seem that hard. Aren't most weapons made of iron, or at least they were?"

"Most weapons can sort of work for a little bit—and everything tends to work on half-bloods, so don't go testing this—but only cold-wrought iron cancels out proper faerie magic and leaves lasting or permanent injuries on them. The more forging—which most metal things need—the less nasty. So there's wrought-iron gates, and there's awkward-looking weapons specifically intended to kill faeries."

Megan thought about that a few seconds. "So, if they heal from everything else, is that what happened to Ashling's wings?"

Lani was quiet for a few seconds, then nodded. "She doesn't like to talk about it. I think she'd even rather think someone mistook her for a butterfly. The Count was able to get her free, but someone knew exactly what they were trying to collect and came prepared."

After thinking about that for a few seconds, looking at the black dot in the sky wheeling back towards them, Megan shuddered, then collected her things to start walking again. "And it was really that big of a thing to the other pixies? It's like she doesn't even look at them."

"Pixies and their relatives are really, really social. That's even how their magic works. One pixie, well, can open some doors and windows and find their way around. Even sidhe lords and ladies usually don't mess with whole glimmers of pixies."

"Glimmers, really?"

"Yes, really. But the point is, pixies fly. Their whole life is based on it. Some of them might have been weirded out by the reminder of vulnerability and actively wanted her out of their pixie games, but mostly she just couldn't keep up."

"And then my dad—?"

"Took her in? Yes. Ashling always loved to explore. Even before it happened, she and the Count were buddies, playing tour guide for each other in Faerie and on Earth. She knew all the pathways, and she'd flown all over the place. So your dad got a new scout, and someone to check on you once in a while."

"He also recognized my excellent tactical skills and the Count's extraordinary knowledge of fashion trends. Before we came along, your dad had no idea how to accessorize properly," Ashling explained as the crow landed on Lani's shoulder.

"Of course," Megan replied, managing a smile and trying not to cringe at the sight of the tattered wings.

On finally reaching the city gates, there was no mistaking it. The high fence was black iron, with pointed tips. Where An Teach Deiridh might have had ivy or thorns, it had vines of additional iron woven throughout. Beyond the fence, she could see some of the buildings shuttered, with dark chains and a lock sealing every entrance.

They stood outside the city for a while, studying the gate. Despite a careful search, there was nothing, literally nothing, to open the gate. Megan looked up at the wall of black iron lattice. The intricate weavings became tighter the higher it climbed. The wind whistled through the cold-wrought gaps. No shrill despairing cry, just a brief indifferent ring. A middle C, maybe, Megan thought. Then she realized Ashling was trying to tell her something.

"I said we've checked," Ashling repeated pronouncedly as the Count found a place on the ground to land. "There's only this one gate, if you can still call it a gate when it's locked this solid. No way in."

Megan gave a short little exhalation, and the wind almost did with her.

"Did you hear something?" she asked. "Something on the wind?"

Lani sighed. "No, Megan. I know that it was awesome that your Dad managed to get in touch, but that was a special case. The winds of faerie magic are very tricky, and they definitely won't work here. We're next to a giant wrought-iron fence. That's really the bulk of a lot of problems. If you heard something, sometimes the wind is just the wind."

And the wind kept whistling, but there was getting into the city to consider.

Everyone looked at each other for a moment. Megan tried to reach toward the gate and then drew back her hand again. If the taste of chewing on aluminum foil could be transferred to the fingers, that would be it. Megan wiggled her hand to circulate the feeling away, happily distracted by the sound of the wind through the now-even-creepier gates.

"The two of you could just fly over," Lani told Ashling and the Count.

"I... I..." Ashling was actually at a loss for words for a moment. "I couldn't get the sword myself. That was part of the point. And the Count doesn't have any hands."

Megan didn't join the conversation, staring and reaching towards the twisted, seamless metal that seemed to be almost some sort of lock without a keyhole. That aluminum feeling in her fingertips was unavoidable. It was almost like a medication overdose concentrated in her skin. A shudder went down her spine, and the wind sang out through the gaps again, one of the brighter versions of the sound.

"There has to be something," Ashling said. "Megan, you seemed to have a knack with that bardic translation book—"

"It's not going to be anything in a book, especially not one the Unseelie King had," Lani argued. "If there's a faerie spell that can open it, that's not tauntingly unavailable, really."

Megan let her do the arguing, her mind seizing on every stepping and skipping whistle of the wind as Lani filtered it out and focused on the main thing going on. It was the story of most of their lives, really.

Megan absently swayed a little. "...C-E-G-E-C-E-G-E-F-A-C-A-C..." she sing-songed smoothly, parroting the notes, but letting them flow together without the long pauses.

And for a moment, the wall seemed to vibrate. And then, the seemingly seamless iron of the lock untwisted itself. The gate opened.

Chapter 19: City in Irons

The girls stood, staring into the open gateway. The wind continued to blow through the wrought-iron bars, but now it was more like a howl than a tuneful hum as it passed through the open gate. The city was no less forbidding with the gate open, just more colorful. Had she not known better, Megan would have thought it abandoned for a few years at most. All over the place, there were faded paints or partial images that had to have once been bright and cheerful, and maybe a little garish. The buildings even seemed to have few sharp edges, and unusual contours and layouts. The only thing close, she realized, was the architecture of a lot of modern concert halls, laid out to produce the best acoustics possible. It was like the entire place had been built to house one great spectacle of sight and sound. Now, all of that crazed precision left the wind echoing through every curve and twist, the whispers and howls echoing back through the streets.

Megan exchanged a look with Lani, both hesitating to push on and step across the threshold into the lost city of iron. As usual, Ashling started on ahead of them.

As the Count started to glide into the city, Ashling shuddered. The Count, noticing, reversed course back through the gates and landed on the ground.

"Count, don't be such a sissy," Ashling hissed through clenched teeth, clinging to the bird's neck. "We have a job to do."

"Caw," the Count replied.

"What? Don't be ridiculous. I'm fine. I will be fine."

"Caw."

"Yes, they do."

"Caw."

"He really, really is."

There was a pause, then a final. "Caw."

"Thank you. It's all okay. Honest, just ... don't brush into anything."

She then visibly tensed further as the crow flew back into the city.

"'He' who?" Megan asked.

"Huh?" Ashling looked at her suddenly. "The Unseelie King, obvi—oh, yeah. You don't speak Corvid."

"Nope. So what about my dad?"

"We were just mentioning him. Because of the job. You know, my cousin Nessa once said... she once said..." Ashling was breathing a little heavier, eyes glancing back to the gates and on to the next iron-wrapped building. Finally, Ashling looked Megan in the eye for a moment. "Well... Nessa and I don't talk anymore. The King and I do. This is worth it."

"I'm sorry," Megan said, as she stepped into the city, following the crow and pixie. "Are you going to be okay in here?"

"I'll be fine," Ashling said, not sounding very convincing as she huddled over more, making sure she had a good grip on the Count. Even so, they flew on.

Some distance into the city, Megan paused. "Did you hear that?"

"How are you hearing anything over the wind?" Lani asked, but paused to listen even so.

After a few moments of the wind's howl, Megan was just starting to think she must have imagined the sound, when it came again. A dull sound of metal on stone that echoed through the corridors, then disappeared into the constant sound around them. "Are you sure there's no one here?" Megan finally asked.

"No one ever said that," Lani responded, looking around through the different passages through the city, trying to figure out where the sound was coming from when it echoed again. "Something keeps preventing people from coming back, after all."

"You're very reassuring."

Lani grabbed hold of Megan's arm, tugging her towards one of the buildings. "I'll keep being reassuring over here, then, away from any of the side streets and alleys."

Ashling and the Count circled higher, surveying the city from the rooftop level, before they finally dove towards Lani, landing on her shoulder. "Incoming!"

"Incoming what?" Megan said, glancing all around.

"I think it might be a giant," Ashling said, focusing on one of the side alleys across the street from them, drawing the girls' attention there.

"I thought there were no more giants," said Megan.

"Tell him," Ashling said, the crow lifting off again as a massive form, at least nine feet tall, tromped into the street, each footfall echoing through the city. As it emerged from the shadows of the alley into the dim light of the open street, Megan could see that the figure seemed to be made all of the same black iron as the gates. Though the construction was frequently somewhat rough compared to most statues she'd seen, the figure still seemed to be made up as a loose interpretation of an armored soldier, down to the sword and shield, bearing an insignia of a rearing horse, permanently attached to the arms.

Megan froze where she was, trying not to draw attention her way, hoping the creature would turn. For a moment, it appeared about to do so, then its gaze fell on the small group. At first, Megan expected it to come running, but instead, it stood tall and tipped its head back. Though its mouth didn't move, the sound that emerged from the statue sounded somewhere between a bellow and a car crash. The sound echoed far louder than its footfalls had, easily carrying over the wind.

All around them, the city started to come alive with new noises. More of the metal-on-stone footfalls came from all directions. "Run!" Ashling shouted, the Count lifting off of Lani's shoulder and leading the way. Once the shout shocked both girls out of staring, they raced for one of the side streets. Hearing crashing behind them, Megan looked back to see the giant statue following, keeping pace with them due to long strides, maybe even gaining a little.

They rounded two more corners trying to lose it and almost ran directly into another, this one with a mountain on its shield. The

Count abruptly swooped upward as the towering form turned a corner just ahead of them. Lani dove to the side to avoid a swipe from its sword. Megan wasn't as agile or lucky, only barely managing to slow down as she collided with a tree-trunk thick leg of iron. She stumbled backwards, barely keeping her feet. Looking back up, she saw the black sword raising. Before it could swing, a tiny black form ridden by a much more colorful one raked past its eyes. The crow's claws didn't do anything to the statue, but the pair got its attention.

The shield came up as the Count was banking upward, the edge smashing into the bird and drawing a scream from Ashling. The crow went into a spin, flapping desperately and trying to regain the skies, while Ashling clung on for dear life. Lani dove, managing to catch them before they hit the ground, though the Count's claws or beak drew a long, bloody gash on her hand and arm as she did. The heroism did buy Megan time to recover. She helped pull Lani back to her feet, and the girls started running again, with Lani holding onto the smaller pair.

There were four more close calls, each new encounter sending them racing down a different alley or side path. Megan paused a few times, looking for signs of anywhere to hide, but all of the doors were chained, and the windows boarded. She never had time to look for long, or truly test any of them, with iron footfalls always sounding like they were just behind them, along with the bellow-crashes that kept announcing their presence any time a new thing found them.

Finally, as she was racing around a corner, almost out of breath, Lani grabbed for her, pulling her to the side. "Over here." Where Lani pointed, there was a window, once shuttered and boarded up like the others, but this one appeared to have been smashed open.

Megan scrambled up into the window and into the building, then accepted Ashling and the Count. As soon as she was able to set the pair down, she reached into the street to help pull her shorter friend in through the window. Neither dared peek out, but they heard crashing footsteps in the street outside. For a few moments, it stilled, though there were more footfalls out there, still coming their way. They held their breath, waiting to see if the thing would see their hiding spot and come crashing through the door or wall. Then the footfalls moved on. A few more came through the area, and each time, they moved on.

Finally, Megan dared to break the silence. "What are those things?"

"Iron golems," came a voice from the other side of the room. "The invulnerable guards of the city."

Chapter 20: Boy out of Time

The boy in the room couldn't have been much older than Megan and Lani, but he was a good bit taller, though clearly slouching from some injury. What drew the attention more than any physical feature, though, was his clothing. He was dressed like something out of a medieval movie, right down to wearing chain mail.

Lani didn't go near him yet, kneeling to tend to Ashling and the Count. Both were conscious and moving, but the Count was favoring one wing, and Ashling was quiet and had a black mark on one leg. Lani was taking both as a bad sign.

"I've no arms," the boy said, holding up his good hand and wincing as it came away from his slumped shoulder.

"Well, you've got them, but one's not looking good," Megan said.

"Weapons, Miss. I have no weapons. My sword broke fighting the golems."

"Oh," Megan said, glancing at the empty sword sheath at his belt. "Weapons probably would have been a good idea."

"Weapons you don't know how to use just encourage you to fight things you probably shouldn't," Lani replied.

"I had a good sword," the boy said. "It didn't do me very much good. The Claiomh Solais, though, should probably work a little better."

"Oh!" Megan exclaimed, "You must be the Queen's other agent. She was asking about you. I'm glad you're alive, but I was expecting someone..."

"A little bit more Fair?" he asked.

"Uh-uh, I knew about the 'human blood' thing, but I'd have figured their first person was older. Or maybe with guns or something instead of a sword."

"Guns really don't work on anything here nearly as well as you'd think they might," Lani said. She looked to the boy, getting in the practical questions Megan was skipping past. "Who are you, anyway? And what do you know about the sword?"

"Justin of Ludlow," he answered, with an obviously painful bow. "I am... I was the squire to Sir Broderick. We came through the portal seeking the Claiomh Solais."

"So where is he?"

"He never made it into Faerie. We had prepared ourselves for the trip, after consulting with numerous scholars on matters of the fae. Horseshoes, iron knives, necklaces of daisies, and, at great expense, plenty of salt."

"Oh, I heard about the salt thing," Megan said. Lani glanced at her with a quirked brow.

"So had we," Justin said. "And we thought we were ready. All we had to do was close our eyes, step through the lodestones, and step back out. As we did, there was a woman's scream and a terrible roar."

"I don't remember that part," Megan said.

"That's because we had a pixie guide," Lani said, still crouched with Ashling, who was half-trying to shoo her away.

"So, what did you see? Who was screaming?" Megan asked, looking back to Justin while Lani helped the pixie and crow.

"There were flames, and the flames just towered. Red-hot... white-hot... Sir Broderick... both his eyes were open. He fell straight for the fire. I managed to wrench myself aside somehow. I still fell. I fell half-blind into smoke and mist and hard earth. Once I could get up, I wandered for hours. Finally, I saw a path bordered by flames again and ran to it. I passed out as I emerged. Finally I woke, collapsed, near a bonfire on the lawn of a castle.

"Balefire," Ashling said, finally joining the conversation. "They're there for a reason, and they're also the reason you don't open your eyes when stepping out of a circle."

Justin nodded, wincing.

"What happened on the lawn?"

"There were two people ... She was like an ethereal saint. He was like an avenging angel—"

"I know, right?" Megan interrupted, then blushed. "Oh, um, sorry."

"She said she'd let me return to the mortal world, but only if I completed a mission."

"Sorry to go back, but where is Ludlow, anyway?" She just had to know. His accent sounded like he was from somewhere between France, Virginia, and another planet.

"England. The Marches, near the Welsh border."

"And what year is it there?" Ashling asked.

"Anno Domini 1389."

Megan blinked. "Oh. Oh, gosh, I hate to break this to you..."

"The Queen already did, Miss. Don't worry. She helped me try to understand the strange future dialect better before she sent me on this quest last fortnight. Not sure why she started with that. The iron golems don't speak it, or speak at all."

"At least you know she intends to keep her word and let you leave."

"Oh, she always keeps her word," Ashling said. "She has to."

"Oh yeah." Megan paused only a moment, her mind still racing around. "So she gave you a mission. The mission was to get the sword? The same thing you'd been trying to do anyway?"

"Well, yes, but not to bring it back to the King anymore—"

Ashling perked up a little. "You've seen the Unseelie King?"

"No," Justin said hurriedly, shaking his head. "No, I absolutely haven't. The King of England wanted to raise everyone's hopes against the machinations of the Lords Appellant—and the bad weather, and the fear the plague will return. Mostly, though, it's politics. Or it was politics." Justin had a strange expression for a moment, which might be understandable when realizing that everyone you know is dead. "Anyway," he continued. "It doesn't matter now. The Queen said I could never re-enter the normal world without first shoving the sword into a stone she showed me."

"Huh. Reverse King Arthur," Megan said. "Of course, we've got a crow instead of an owl."

Justin looked puzzled. "What do owls have to do with King Arthur?"

"Let's just not talk about owls," Lani said. "So, the sword."

"Yes, the sword. I've seen it," Justin said. "I'm in no shape to make another attempt. They keep it well guarded. Most of the golems don't seem very intelligent. Distractions worked well. The four guarding the sword, however, seemed to have different instructions, or better magic animating them. They won't leave the sword alone. That made it harder to take, but, thankfully, made them easier to escape, too." He said, glancing at his injured arm.

"So, at least we have a better idea what we're up against," Lani said. "We're going to need a plan. But we have some time. I hope you don't mind us inserting ourselves into the mission, Justin, but we're after the same thing. It seems like the best idea."

"It does," Justin agreed. "As soon as I can move my arm enough to fight."

After checking on Ashling one more time, Lani crossed the room. "Let me take a look at it."

Chapter 21: Plans of Attack

Megan moved over to Ashling and settled down, now that she was fairly sure the golems weren't paying the damaged window any attention. She noticed the black mark. The thoughts of mention of iron and Ashling's damaged wings sprang quickly to mind. "Is that...?" she started, not precisely sure what to even ask.

"Just iron burn," Ashling replied. "It barely touched me. It will heal, eventually, when we're out of the city."

"So all you have to do is touch it?"

"Not as bad," Ashling agreed. "But yes, if the iron is pure enough, just touching it hurts. This is sort of like, I guess, if you touched something red-hot. Which you really shouldn't do, by the way." She sounded like she was speaking from experience.

"I'll keep it in mind," Megan assured her. "How is the Count?"

The crow cawed, Megan glanced at him, then back to Ashling. "He says he'll probably be able to fly in a day or two. Maneuvering very well might be longer, though."

Lani sighed, as she went through her pack for bandages. "We only have a couple of days. Most of our food is still in Cassia's chariot."

"Oh yeah," Megan said. She looked to Justin. "So you got away from the hounds without someone to distract them?"

"...Not exactly."

"Not exactly someone?"

"Not exactly 'got away.' I was brought up that it's better to ask permission than run screaming."

Megan looked at Justin for a moment. "So you just asked the giant monster dogs nicely to let you through?"

"No. I asked the Huntsman." His good hand attempted to help Lani hold the bandages as she wound them into a brace for his bad arm.

"Tall guy? Scary Looking? Horns?" Megan asked.

"You've met him, then?"

"No, I saw the paintings of the hunt and didn't especially want to meet anyone in them."

"Well, I found him, introduced myself, explained whom I'd served under and who commissioned me, and asked his leave to cross his lands in my own hunt."

"And that's not cheating?"

"... It's the exact opposite of cheating, Miss. That's how it's done when you hunt across someone else's land. And I was hunting, after a fashion."

"And the scary faerie guy with the horns and the black horse and a pack of dogs almost as big, he just said 'okay'?" Megan asked.

"He granted the request, yes. Seemed like being asked was a bit novel."

"Did he give you a ride across the unfordable river, too?"

"No, had to swim that."

"You swam? But there were rapids with monster fish and migratory whirlpools!"

If not for the all the effort he and Lani were putting into immobilizing his arm, Justin would probably have shrugged again. "I watched the currents for two days to find the most possible crossing-point. Fish are the least active at high noon, so that's when I swam. Very hard."

"And then you climbed through the plains and hills without the dogs bothering you, and then you heard the song—"

"What song?"

"On the wind. To open the gate."

"There's a lot of sound on the wind, Miss. I didn't see any way of opening that gate."

"But you're in here."

"I climbed the fence."

"You just... climbed it?" Megan was blinking.

"Okay, as soon as your good hand's free, I want to shake it," Lani said, smiling as she finished wrapping his arm tight.

"But what about the gross hazy feeling?" Megan could not get over the idea of climbing that huge, disgusting fence.

"You've lost me, Miss. I... take it you're... of the Fair Folk, then?"

"Half," Lani said. "She's the Unseelie King's daughter."

"Oh." Now Justin actually got to look surprised. "Pleasure to meet you, Highness."

"Just Megan, please."

"Megan then," he said, a little confused, but offering his good hand to Lani when she finished binding his shield arm. "The fence was a hard climb, to be sure, but I'm not ... that is, I'm quite, quite mortal. I don't think it was meant to keep humans out. On the other hand, I was definitely not going to get back out with the bad shoulder."

"And a couple of cracked ribs, I think," Lani added. "Your shoulder was dislocated. Just a little, so hopefully it will heal fast. You won't be able to use it at all for a while though, so I've got it as secure as I could with the supplies we have."

"My thanks."

Megan smiled a little. "Thinking of going pre-med instead of majoring in engineering now?"

Lani smiled back. "You canceling art school plans because you sang a gate open? The human body's just another machine. Except when it's not." She looked back to Justin. "You're welcome."

The boy nodded, still trying to take a lot in. "When we've rested, I can guide you to the sword. We'll need a plan, though."

"Even with one arm, I think Justin should get the sword," Lani said. "He actually knows how to use one, and has the best chance to hurt the golems with it."

"He won't be able to run much, though. And there's a lot of golems," Megan said. "One of us should probably try to get it, and the others can make a distraction to draw them as far away as we can get them? Once he has the sword, hopefully it will be able to damage them."

"Agreed," Justin said. "They're slow enough that with a working weapon, I think I can best one of them at a time. The problems were numbers and having nothing that threatened them."

Megan looked towards where Ashling was resting, nestled up against the Count. "Are you two going to be in any shape to help with the distraction? I don't want you to hurt yourselves worse."

"We'll manage," Ashling said. "After all, you need us."

Megan sat down next to Ashling, and carefully, after making sure the bird didn't seem to object, stroked the crow's headfeathers a little. "Thank you. Both of you. I know you really care about my dad."

"Yeah, well, he's care-about-able." Ashling smiled. "Starting to think it runs in the family. And Lani is such a team player. And you've got to realize, the Count really likes teams. Hates doing without them. He's attempted murder a few times, but it never worked out."

As Megan felt the crow sigh under her fingers, she tried to parse that sentence.

"Because…no other crows showed up to be in the murder?"

"Obviously."

"Yes. Obviously."

Lani wanted them all to try sleeping at that point, but Megan gave up on that fairly quickly. While none of the iron giants ever tried to break into their shelter, the loud metal-on-stone noise passing by every hour or so not only woke her, but kept her on edge until it passed. Each time, just as exhaustion started to push her to sleep, the noise would arise again, bringing her back to paranoid alertness. Looking around, the others weren't faring much better. Justin often seemed the closest to drifting off, but the binding on his arm made any position awkward.

Their basic plan didn't help Megan relax any either, particularly with half of the group injured. No one was able to come up with anything better than 'grab the sword and run during a distraction,' though, and they weren't likely to when they couldn't even sleep. At least it was simple.

After the passage of yet another golem, after she was sure no one was asleep, and no one looked likely to change that, she finally stood and headed for the window, surveying the city outside. "If the

Count can fly, we should start moving as soon as it's light enough to see."

"We need to rest and heal," Lani said. "We have a couple of days' supplies."

"Do you feel any better rested? And Ashling is getting worse, not better. Besides, in two days, we might be healed more; we might not, but I'll definitely be going stir crazy." It might just have been the sleep deprivation, but Megan could almost feel the city sapping her strength as well. "Let's do this."

While the teens looked between each other, Ashling spoke to the crow. Finally, the Count tested his wings, hopped a couple of times, and then flew to Megan's shoulder. "He says he can fly, but maybe not while carrying me." She looked to Megan. "Can I have the left shoulder?"

"Okay," Megan said, picking the pixie up gently.

"I guess I'm running for the sword, then?" Lani asked.

"You're faster than I am. You've proven that a couple of times. Ashling, the Count, and I will work on the distraction."

"And what am I to do?" Justin asked.

"Stay out of the way, and Lani will get you the sword. Then it will be up to you to get them off of us."

"I'll be ready."

Chapter 22: The Sword is Drawn

At first light, they followed Justin's directions through the city, having to backtrack and change directions at the sight of various golems. As they got closer to the center of the city, the patrols grew more frequent. By hugging buildings and scouting as best they could, they managed to avoid any more chases, but it was slow going, and there were a lot more close calls than Megan was remotely comfortable with.

At last, Justin stopped them. "Around the next corner, you'll be able to see the great hall. All of the doors have been torn off and the golems come and go. Pay very close attention to where the doors are and don't let them corner you. They'll try."

"How reassuring. So the sword is in there?" Lani asked.

"Laid across the arms of the great chair in the main hall," Justin said. "Just as much of a taunt as the rest of this place. Also easy to guard. There's four golems there. Two of them gave chase, two remained on watch. More came when they called. We will need to make this quick."

"And indoors, the Count won't have as much room to fly out of reach," Megan said, starting to turn the corner anyway, with Ashling sitting astride one shoulder, the crow perched on the other. "If we need to hurry, let's hurry."

Justin reached out, pulling her back. "Wait, time the patrols."

She watched from around the corner, until a golem tromped by their hiding spot. Megan couldn't help reflecting that the tower emblazoned on its shield looked a little like a rook in chess. It paused there for a moment, but showed no sign of turning towards them, and eventually began walking again. "Now," Justin whispered, starting around the corner. Following his lead, the others quietly paced several yards behind the tower-golem, following it into the building before ducking into an alcove to hide.

"Right... they travel one at a time. And make a lot of noise. Can I shake your hand again, for good measure?" Lani asked.

"There will be more than one soon enough," Justin replied, instinctively reaching for the sheath that no longer held a sword.

The tower-golem disappeared down a hallway. They could hear more footsteps echoing down other halls, and even the sound of footfalls from the next floor up. For a few moments, all the different footfalls in all directions tested Megan's nerves. She started entertaining the thought of ducking back out the door.

Justin led the way a short time further, with the group doing their best to remain near hiding places, having to duck back a few times to avoid being spotted, waiting there nervously until the golems passed. Finally, he gestured to a wide passage where double doors used to stand. "There."

Through the doorway they could see the room he'd described, great chair and all. Otherwise, Megan couldn't help but notice the similarities between the rest of the room and some of Seattle's concert halls. A large part of the room was left open for dancing or spectating, but there was still plenty of space for a truly grand stage. The red curtains of the stage were even mostly preserved through whatever odd effect kept most of the city intact, though they were tattered and threadbare.

The rest of the room was a sight. All over the stage, and particularly on the floor, there was the remains of all manner of instruments and stage props. Most of the cloth, wood, and paper had disintegrated, but there were a few hints of those. There was plenty of metal, however, with the twisted frames of horns mingled with strings and struts, strewn among the wrecked frames of drums, with the odd bits of old costumes, prop weapons and now-unidentifiable things scattered among them. While most of the city was left to simply stand as a tortured reminder of what it had been, this place seemed intentionally ransacked and the contents destroyed and discarded. Among the wreckage were several clear lanes, where the golems passed through the room, from the doors to the grand chair of the lord of the hall.

As promised, laid across the arms of the chair, as if in waiting for the lord's return, was a sheathed sword with a jeweled hilt. Also as promised, four golems stood sentry, one at each corner of the massive chair. One carried a shield with a hand symbol on it, one with a boot. A large, singular eye was emblazoned on each of the shields of the two behind them.

Megan started into the room with the pixie on one shoulder and the crow on the other. She darted towards the throne, picking up speed as she went.

It took only a few moments before the golems took notice, all four turning their heads in her direction in an eerie unison. The two at the back raised their heads, starting into the grating bellow she'd heard on the first encounter. The other pair turned, continuing to move in almost perfect symmetry, raising their swords, lowering their shields and advancing on her. Megan let them get a little closer, then turned, racing back for the door out of the room.

To her surprise, when she turned, she saw Lani and Justin rushing into the room coming towards her and waving frantically. Before she could turn around, she saw the reason for their alarm. The tower-golem was advancing on the door. When it arrived just behind Lani and Justin, it crouched and raised its shield, blocking the exit and trapping them in the room.

Megan spun again, seeing the hand-golem and the boot-golem coming at her along the path through the wreckage. After a moment of hesitation, she rushed towards the stage, risking the minefield of ruined instruments and stage props. She heard the sound of crunching metal all too close behind her, and could see the others not far off in her peripheral vision. Lani seemed to be navigating the garbage well enough, but Justin nearly fell when he stepped on the remains of a drum, catching his balance, but allowing the hand-golem to close a lot of the distance while he did so.

"Split up!" Megan yelled. "They can only follow two of us, someone can try to get the sword." It seemed like their best bet on the spur of the moment.

Justin ducked under a swing of a sword, then headed back towards the door, trying to draw his attacker away from the girls. Lani took off to the left, nimbly moving through the wreckage.

Drawing a mixture of chagrin and relief at once, the boot-golem stayed on Megan's heels.

"Get to the stage!" Ashling yelled in her ear. As she offered her guidance, the Count lifted off Megan's shoulder, flying towards the golem pursuing Justin. Megan almost lost her balance, sliding on some old strings left on the floor. As she got her leg unensnared from the wires of the old lute, they cut into her ankle. The bleeding wound threw off Megan's stride even as she started running. In the process of catching herself, Ashling went pitching forward off of Megan's shoulder. Megan paused to grab for her, but Ashling gestured backwards. "Look out!"

Megan glanced back in time to sidestep. The boot-golem's sword cleaved deep into the floor next to her. While it was recovering, Ashling dove back towards Megan, starting to climb her pants leg until Megan could get a hand on her.

"I'll just slow you down. Throw me!" Ashling shouted. Megan was about to protest, but the sword had been pulled free, and was coming up for another swing. She desperately threw the pixie towards the curtains as hard as she could, then ran for the stage. The sword crashed down just behind her, barely missing her leg, buying her another moment when the golem had to remove its blade from the floor.

Managing to pick her pace back up, she tried to leap onto the stage, failing to clear it by inches and ending up sprawling forward. She turned over to see a sword coming down at her, and desperately rolled to one side, avoiding a swing that cut deep into the stage. The giant pulled the blade free, and she dove out of reach as the next swing came at her. The golem pursued, the front of the stage collapsing under its weight with each step towards her.

"Banzai!" came a voice from above. Ashling, having pulled or cut a portion of the curtain free, clutched it as she dove toward the boot-golem, pulling more of the ragged red fabric down with her, tattered wings flapping furiously to attempt any control over her descent. The golem looked up, to see a wave of red coming down at it. It thrust its sword upward, the blade tearing through the fabric and just missing Ashling. A moment later, the pixie hit the stage, stunned. The golem was staggering, head and sword arm entangled in the fabric for the moment. Megan took the opportunity, scooping up Ashling on her way to going running towards Justin.

While Megan had been on her own chase, the hand-golem had been working to herd Justin back towards the tower-golem at the door. Every time it came too close, the crow flapped past its eyes, drawing the hand-golem's attention. Still, the squire was running out of room.

Megan grabbed for one of the ruined horns, flinging it at the hand-golem. The metal instrument rang off the back of its head, causing it to turn enough to look her way. Justin took the opportunity to run towards her, past the golem's shield arm.

When she spun back around to flee the hand-golem, now chasing them both, she saw the boot-golem pulling free from the curtain in one corner. On the other side of the room, Lani was playing chicken with the eye-golems, ducking into reach, then back out when they swung their swords. Try as she might, she couldn't draw them away from the great chair, though it also meant that, as long as nothing else came for her, Lani was safe from a certain distance away. That didn't help in getting to the sword, though.

"Go and help her," Justin said. "Get the sword."

"What about you?" Megan asked, out of breath.

"I have an idea."

Megan nodded, racing back for the throne and Lani. She pulled up short, just out of reach of the swords, staring up at the twin sentries.

"Any more ideas?" Lani asked.

"Just one. You go left; I go right," Megan said, setting Ashling down. "She goes for the sword."

"What?" Lani asked, looking at her incredulously. "How is she going to do anything with it?"

"Trust me. Ashling, just try to shove it this way."

The pixie focused on the sword. "Ready when you are."

"We have to buy her time," Megan said. "Keep them busy."

Both girls rushed forward, then charged to either side, drawing the eye-golems while Ashling rushed forward, climbing the side of the throne.

On the main floor, Justin ran from the hand-golem, slowed down by his injuries, but staying just ahead of it. He set his sights on the boot-golem as the curtain fell to the floor at its feet. He ran directly at it, the boot-golem readying its sword as its fellow chased the squire towards it. Near the last second, he gestured towards the pursuing golem's head. "Count!"

The bird swooped past the eyes of the hand-golem, distracting it for a moment. At the last second, Justin dropped, sliding along the floor just under the boot-golem's swing. He lay there, wincing and glancing back. Distracted by the Count, and with a lot of forward momentum already, the hand-golem failed to stop in time and crashed into the boot-golem, still off-balance from the swing at Justin. Both crashed to the floor—Justin barely managed to roll out from under them before they fell, gritting his teeth hard to avoid crying out as he rolled over his injured shoulder. Justin pulled himself to his feet, getting a little more distance before the golems untangled themselves.

Megan and Lani feinted towards the throne in turns, trying to hold the attention of the eye-golems. After a hard swing that Megan barely evaded, she ran behind the great chair while her attacker freed his sword from the floor. He recovered faster than she expected, and all she could do was drop to the ground under a new swing that crashed into the back of the chair. To Megan's surprise, the great chair held with only a small nick, though the blow threw up sparks. The impact also rattled the chair enough that Ashling staggered, almost tumbling off of the front of the chair before she recovered her balance amidst furious flapping. The pixie grabbed for one of the straps on the hilt and began pulling as hard as she could, budging the sword an inch at a time.

Seeing what had happened, Lani darted for Megan, trying to egg the right eye-golem to swing at her and giving Megan a moment to recover. Rather than trying to get to her feet, having seen the chair take the hit, Megan scrambled underneath it. Lani's game of chicken with the right eye-golem bought Megan time, but it also ended up leaving Lani vulnerable to a swing from the left eye-golem when she dodged a strike from the right. Though she managed to twist out of the way of the worst of it, Lani still fell with a vicious cut to her side, just under her ribcage. The sword swing's momentum carried it into the back of the throne, rattling the chair again, sending Ashling and the sword tumbling off of it this time.

While the golems were distracted, noticing the sword and colorful butterfly wings falling, Megan grabbed for Lani's leg, pulling her under the chair. She turned just in time to see a golem stepping into a swing at Ashling as the pixie strained at pulling the blade across the dais. "Ashling!" she called a warning. The pixie looked up in time to see the attack, diving out of the way, but leaving the sword behind. Past them, she could see the hand-golem and the boot-golem pulling themselves back to their feet, sights set on Justin again.

With the eye-golems looking at Ashling, Megan left Lani for the moment and crawled out from under the chair, grabbing for the sword. The movement drew renewed attention, one of the golems looking away from Ashling and taking a swing at Megan. Holding the sheathed blade, she dove out onto the floor, rolling away painfully as she landed amidst the wreckage in the room. For a moment, she nearly drew the sword, but looked back, to see the guardians once again standing, threatening and warning her away from the chair, but not pursuing even though she had the blade. While their attention was on Megan, Lani crawled out from under the back, and snuck behind the eye-golems, clutching at her side.

"Justin!" Megan shouted, drawing the attention of everyone in the room. As the boot-golem turned back to pursue her, Megan flung the sword.

It wasn't a particularly good throw, clattering to the ground several feet short. Both Justin and the hand-golem glanced at the blade, and the squire went for it as the golem struck. Megan screwed her eyes shut.

She opened them in time to see all attention shifted back towards Justin where he lay, good hand holding the sword. Though the hand-golem's strike had smashed him to the floor, he'd gotten the sheathed blade between himself and the iron edge of the sword. Neither sword nor sheath was damaged, keeping him from being cut in two.

Justin did his best to get back to his feet, but was unable to draw the sword with one hand. He managed to interpose it again as the golem struck, hitting the sword and smashing it back against Justin's chest. Instead of being cut, the Claiomh Solais held, but Justin was pitched back towards Megan, flying through the air before he rolled to a stop at her feet.

"Are you all right?" Megan asked, trying to help him back to his feet.

"Milad—Megan, grab the sheath, I need a sword." he grunted back, struggling back to his feet as the hand-and boot-golems advanced, trying to herd the pair back towards the guardians at the throne.

Megan grabbed on with both hands, and Justin pulled the sword free. As it was drawn, there was a flash of blue light. Holding a sword of pure white metal, wreathed in blue flames, Justin stepped up to defend Megan as the golems bore down on him.

Chapter 23: A Clash of Swords

The golems paused as if reassessing their opponent, then started in motion again. Justin moved to one side, moving inside the reach of the next sword-swing, lashing out with the magic sword towards the boot-golem's leg.

The metal impacted with a resounding clang, leaving a shallow scar in the metal of the golem's leg. The golem's own sword came down without a hitch, and Justin barely got the Claiomh Solais up in time to block just enough to let him stagger out of the way.

Megan ran to try to support Lani, then looked to Justin as he made two more swipes at the golems, the impacts ringing off their legs.

"Shouldn't that have, you know, cut its leg off or something?" Megan asked Lani.

"You'd think, but we have to focus. The maidens need to go rescue the brave knight now."

"Right," Megan agreed, searching for a few moments until she found Ashling, scooping up the exhausted pixie and holding on.

Justin's resistance and the flaming sword at least kept the pair of golems' attention, but he still had no luck. Each time, he had to dodge out of the way of the counterattacks quickly.

"It's not working," Lani yelled as they rushed for him. "Run!"

Justin fended off another attack, staggering under the impact, but at least much better suited to fighting now that he had the invulnerable blade. As soon as he caught his balance, Justin received a brief respite when the Count dive-bombed the hand-golem. The crow was barely able to bank out of the way of its next swing. As Justin ran past the distracted golem to join the girls, the Count flew after them, having to flap hard just to regain enough altitude to stay off the floor.

"Where to?" Megan said as they sprinted, her glance at the door not only confirming that it was still blocked, but that behind the tower-golem, reinforcements were arriving. The room would likely be full of golems soon.

"The stage!" Lani yelled, running ahead at the damaged stage and pulling herself up onto it.

"We'll be trapped!" Megan called after her, but she followed anyway, helping Justin up. The delay almost cost both of them, as a sword came crashing down on the floor just behind them.

"No, we won't. I have a magic trick!" Lani called, heading for the dressing room, the door hanging from one hinge.

"I thought faerie magic wouldn't work." Megan said, rushing through the door after her.

Lani waved Justin and the Count through. "Sure, but Houdini will work fine. Justin, attack."

"But the golems are..."

"Yes, yes," Lani agreed. "But the back wall here is just wood."

By the time the golems smashed through the wall to the dressing room, they found a hole carved into the back wall.

Navigating through the hall and back into the streets wasn't easy, with quite a few of the golems having been drawn by the grating bellows. Most of them had been drawn to the main hall, but a few still patrolled. Finding the doorways blocked, with another bellow from a sentry setting new golems chasing them, the group ran up the stairs, managing to duck into an empty side room just at the top before another golem could reach them and trap them on the stairs.

Lani ran to the window, checking to make sure the outside was clear before Justin smashed through it with the sword. With more golems in pursuit, they jumped out the window, each wincing from the impact on injuries before sprinting for the nearest alleyway.

After a few more twists and turns, the sounds of golem footsteps faded behind them. Justin finally chanced smashing out another window, before he accepted help climbing through. Once inside, the group collapsed, almost as one, trying to catch their breath. They only really relaxed at all, though, once the first golem patrols passed by them, ignoring the broken window.

As soon as she'd caught her breath enough, Lani turned to Megan. "How did you know about the sword and the chair?"

"What about them?"

"That they'd keep guarding the chair, and not chase us after we got the sword?"

"Oh, that. It was a guess. The Queen's story sounded like the sword might have been put there later. So when they were built, the golems were like the rest of this place—just a taunt. Their job was guarding the ruler's chair or whatever. Later, whoever brought the sword in just figured they could get two things guarded with one trick."

"Good guess."

"Speaking of questions," Megan said, glancing at Justin, "Why do you keep going for their legs? You're tall-ish."

"I know I'm tall. But that's how it's done! Always go for the legs with a sword like this."

Well, granted, he was the expert on what to do with a sword. "Why?"

"Less armor there."

Megan paused, blinking. "Justin, they're solid metal robots."

"I noticed," he agreed, re-sheathing the sword.

"So it won't cut them. What now?" Megan asked.

Lani and Justin exchanged a glance, then nodded at one another at some unspoken, practical-person agreement. "We get bandaged up and walk out of the city," Lani said. "We have what we came for."

"Oh...right." Megan said, before moving to help bandage Lani's side first.

With Lani's side bound, Megan's leg bandaged, Justin's arm sling adjusted and rewrapped, and Ashling and the Count on Megan's shoulders, they made their way to the city gates again. This time, while noises echoed through the streets still, they didn't have any more close calls, or even see any of the golems.

Their luck ran out when they finally came within sight of the gates. Thankfully, they saw the golems before they were seen, and ducked back around a corner. Peering out, they were able to see where the creatures had gone. They were lined up along the fence, one every twenty-five feet or so, standing sentry.

"What are they doing?" Megan asked.

"We're not just pests anymore. Someone invaded the main hall and escaped," Lani said. "They're making sure no one gets out."

Chapter 24: Escape from Findias

The group retreated back to a building to hide. Where before, the city had been nerve-wracking with all the noise, now, the eerie silence, broken up only by the singing wind, was almost worse.

"So we're trapped?" Megan asked, sitting up against one wall, with Ashling and the Count nestled together next to her. "What do we do now?"

"Try to get some sleep," Lani answered. "Maybe they'll move if we wait long enough."

Megan looked skeptical. "I guess we'll know if they do." For a while, she sat awake, listening for any sound of new noise, and eventually drifted to sleep, with the song on the wind playing over and over in her mind.

Megan woke up to searing pain in her leg. A quick examination revealed that the cuts had puffed up and grown angrier under the bandages, and her calf was swollen. She managed to stifle the sounds of pain, but the noise still woke Ashling next to her. Up close, the pixie looked paler—more of a dull yellow—and thinner than Megan remembered. Her wings drooped, and her eyes were sunken. Now, Megan had no question: the city was having an effect on the pixie.

A look around the rest of the room revealed Lani and Justin, sitting together talking in one corner, where Lani had stacked up some of her supplies. Graffiti, mostly equations, covered the walls.

Megan sat up, groaning as she did so, drawing attention in her direction. Trying to ignore the injury, she looked at the graffiti, then at Lani. "That is the nerdiest gang sign ever."

"Gang sign?" Justin asked, looking between the girls. Megan noticed the glint of the jeweled hilt of the Sword of Light, now replacing the empty sheath on Justin's belt.

Lani sighed. "To avoid letting your induced grasp of modern English get led astray, I should mention that technically, no gang sign is involved. That's hand signals. This would be tagging."

"Right, right," Megan said. "He can see gang sign when he sees you and Kerr."

"Never mind that," Lani said, looking exhausted. The deep cut in her side looked worse than Megan's ankle, even with the heavy bandaging they'd managed. "I think we have a plan."

Megan glanced at Ashling, then back to Lani. "I think, whatever it is, we need to try it, and soon. Going to tell me what the math homework is all about?"

"Engineering as it applies to classical mythology," Lani said. "Every invulnerable thing in a story has a weak spot. If you know it, and have the right weapon, you can beat them."

"So we're going to stab them in the heels?"

"Right principle, wrong mythology. I spent the night trying to reverse engineer them."

"I didn't think faerie magic would work here."

"Menehune, we're not quite as vulnerable to iron as the Celtic fae. It's actually still really unpleasant here, but I think I still made it work, once you got to sleep. My conclusion is that it's best to go for the eye."

"So what do we do?"

"We need bait, and then we need Justin."

Megan was about to speak up when Ashling interjected. "The Count and I are agreed: we're the bait."

"Caw."

"You're both hurt. You could just get out of here now," Megan said. "I should do it."

"On that leg? And Lani can't do it either. Not all cut open. We're not leaving until you do. What do we need to do?"

Lani looked about to object, then changed her mind. "Get one of them to swing down at you, we need to get the head within Justin's sword reach. Are you sure the Count can fly with you on his back?"

"Caw, caw."

"He says that last time he flew without me, I almost got myself killed, so we're sticking together, bad wing or no. He also mentioned that Justin snores. And recited his favorite limerick to get his spirits up."

Megan glanced at Ashling. "Really, he said all that?"

"Corvid is a very efficient language," Ashling explained. "It's like Spanish that way."

"Corvid is like Spanish?"

"Close cousins, yes. After all, he is named in honor of Alvaro Queipo de Llano, Count of Toreno."

Megan opened her mouth to mention her father's explanation of the name, then thought better of it, guessing that the pixie was trying to put on a brave face of normality. "I see. Okay, so what do we do?"

Lani checked her own bandages one more time, then started for the smashed-open window. "We run as best we can and keep running until we're out of the city. I don't think they'll follow us, based on your little trick with the golems and the chair."

"Okay, got it," Megan said, limping after Lani. "I hope you're right."

"So do I," Lani agreed, giving Megan a brief hug. "If not, we try to make sure someone gets away with the sword, agreed?"

"Agreed," Justin answered, following them out through the window.

Megan took a deep breath, not at all liking the notion of leaving anyone behind. "Agreed." There were bigger things at stake.

At first, the Count looked to be unsteady in the air, wavering in flight and flapping more than usual, but after circling a couple of times, he finally seemed to have the hang of it and headed for the main gate.

As soon as they approached the gates, the grating shouts began. The two golems standing sentry near the gate, each with a tower on their shield, closed to block the path out of the city. Others began stomping towards the group to surround them as they neared the gate.

Ashling gestured, and the Count dove at one of them. The golem's initial swipe at the crow missed, but the bird didn't climb, instead, landing on the ground in front of the tower-golems. The one on the right swung his sword downward. The blow came close enough to send feathers flying, but the Count had managed to take off just in time to avoid anything more serious.

Justin charged while the golem had its sword buried in the stone walk, then thrust upward, burying the flaming sword into the golem's eye. The eyeball shattered like glass, and a burst of blue flame shot into the socket. Something inside seemed to be still flaming as the golem staggered backwards, then fell over, unmoving.

"Run!" Lani shouted, as golems closed in on their flanks. Megan didn't need to be told twice, sprinting as hard as her leg allowed towards the gate, despite the pain.

Justin held his ground against the remaining tower-golem. It raised its sword for him and slashed downward. Justin side-stepped the blow, the sword coming down an inch from him. Then he thrust the Sword of Light upward, striking the eye, with the same results as before.

He spun, readying himself for more golems. Megan ran by him first, rushing out of the gates, then Lani followed, clutching at her side. Justin started backing towards the gates, defending the retreat.

He was almost to the gates when a golem caught up to him. He blocked the blow with his sword, only to have it smashed back into his chest. The force of the blow lifted him off his feet and through the air. He hit the ground and, unable to get back to his feet before they caught up, rolled out of the way as another sword blow hit where he'd been lying. He started trying to get back up and ready to fight, when he felt a hand on his shoulder.

"Justin, we made it," Megan said, looking at the line of golems stopped at the gate, watching, but not moving. Then a panicked realization hit her. "We need to go back for..." Her words cut off as the Count flew over the gate, flapping hard to keep control as he descended, and landed on Megan's shoulder. "Right. Bird," Megan finished.

"We need to keep moving," Lani said. "We have a long trip ahead of us, and not many supplies left. Besides, I know they're stopped right now, but..."

"But I'm not going to feel any better until the city is out of sight either," Megan said, trying to help Lani move with as little stress on her side as possible, while Justin moved to help take some weight off of Megan's leg. "But what do we do about the dogs?"

"I remembered to ask for passage both ways," Justin said.

"Of course you did."

Chapter 25: Regrouping

Megan's leg was throbbing as she tried to keep supporting Lani on the hike down. She was wondering just how much longer Justin was going to last trying to climb one-handed when Ashling shouted, "Okay, we're far enough from the city now!"

"Glad to see that you're feeling better," Megan muttered. The black mark on Ashling's leg had faded to light gray.

"Yep! Your turn. Sit down and get the music book out of the bag. There's a page the king probably still has bookmarked. It might help."

Everyone sat down. Megan got out the book and opened it. "There's...two ribbons and a piece of paper shoved in the book. Which page do you mean?"

"Probably the one marked with the Medal of Honor ribbon."

"My dad uses somebody's Medal of Honor as a bookmark?"

"His library matters to him. He likes bookmarks that mattered to somebody. Try reading the song."

"This is a good time for music lessons?"

"Bardic magic is some impressive stuff. I don't have the knack, but you do. And I've known some other bards, so ..."

"You've known some... how old are you, anyway?"

"As old as the trees... well, as old as some young trees. But totally trees that count as trees. Not saplings anymore."

"I'm sorry I asked."

Megan looked at the words and notes on the marked page and began carefully singing them. The words weren't that hard to pronounce at all, once she got into the groove of it. She almost felt like she knew what they meant, even though she didn't speak the language at all. It felt somewhere between a lullaby and a work-song. When she finally looked at Justin, Megan thought for a moment that he was going to fall asleep as the expression on his face shifted. Trying to analyze it, it took her a minute to realize she hadn't yet seen him when he wasn't in pain.

With a little more singing, while her leg remained swollen and scratched, the intensity of the wounds decreased, not looking as angry. The pain also lessened considerably. Lani didn't just look more relaxed: when the pain eased, she started to drift off almost right away.

"Are there going to be a lot more of these music lessons?" Megan asked Ashling.

"You bet!"

"So what's the first rule of barding?"

"Providing excellent protection to your horse," Ashling replied immediately.

"Huh?"

"The second rule is a lot more helpful," Ashling acknowledged. "That's about inspiration."

The walk was much easier after that. Not being chased certainly helped. Their first encounter with the dogs initially put Megan on edge, but Justin just walked up, extending a hand. The lead hound sniffed at him, then bounded away, followed by the rest of his pack. After that, there were no more difficulties, and no other packs approached them.

When they finally reached the unfordable river, the makeshift ramp Cassia had laid on the Hounds' side of the bridge had been knocked over. Megan took a deep breath and reminded herself that Cassia was probably fine. She also had to remind herself that they hadn't run out on her and the cats. Megan didn't want to have run out on anyone.

As they carefully clutched the ropes and inched their way across the bridge, Megan looked up enough to notice smoke in the distance. Not a lot and not very far.

"What do you think that is?" she asked.

"Campfire, maybe," said Justin, moving carefully along the ropes, taking twice as long as the girls due to his injury, but looking glad to not be swimming.

From there, it didn't take long to find the source of the smoke. Cassia and the cats had settled on the far bank and made a small camp. All of them looked the worse for their earlier encounter, still scratched and bruised, but alive. The chariot looked the worst of all. When they first walked into camp, Cassia was working on replacing a broken axle with limited luck. "I'll fix it tonight." Lani offered.

Cassia grinned wide, leaping to her feet and limping over to give Lani a hug, then Megan. "Gently." Lani groaned, clutching at her side again. Both cats rose, Jude heavily favoring a front leg as they made their way over to nose at the girls and greet them as well.

After the hugs, Cassia looked at Justin. "And who is this? What have you girls been up to? What's with the costume? Do I need to get out some fives?"

Lani sighed, but Justin just glanced at her oddly at the stream of questions. "Justin of Ludlow," he replied, with a slightly awkward bow. "You're wounded. The packs?"

Cassia grinned. "Nothing you can't kiss and make better, handsome." That time, Justin blushed brightly. Cassia took the opportunity to press her momentary advantage and looked to Megan. "You know what they say about Ludlow boys, right?"

"That they're very responsible and hardworking," Lani interrupted, narrowing her eyes at Cassia, moving to rest a hand on Justin's shoulder. "Especially by people who want their chariot fixed."

Cassia sighed. "Yes, yes. That was it. Very hardworking."

"So what was your plan for now, Justin?" Megan asked, eager to change the subject.

"My original plan was to go home, hear people cheer, see the Lords Appellant quake in their expensive and overly clean boots, and be set for life. Now, it's to fulfill my agreement with the Queen by putting the sword in the stone, and then…figure out what happens next."

"I don't see how the sword's going to help us save Ric if we stick it in a rock," Cassia pointed out.

"It'll be fine," Megan insisted. "We'll do the deal and then use it to save my dad. We can't leave Justin stuck here." She settled in by the fire to enjoy her first hot food in some time and to read through the music book more for as long as there was light, occasionally asking Ashling questions. The pixie always answered, but in her typical fashion. Nonetheless, Megan was pretty sure she was getting the general idea.

Lani examined the chariot, making notes, and then had food before a long nap, not trying to do any work while people were awake. Cassia and Justin talked over dinner. Megan didn't catch much of it, but there was some discussion of swordplay and life in other centuries—in between Cassia trying to draw more blushing, and Justin fending off the feigned advances.

Finally, Megan settled in to sleep, as did the others, with Lani waking up to go to work on the chariot.

They were awakened by Maxwell's warning snarl, Jude joining in moments later. Megan clambered to her unsteady feet, looking around for the disturbance. Her first impression in the dim light of early morning was of a small, glowing ball of light floating nearby. A rustle and splash drew her eyes to the water's edge, where a tall, gangly woman with grayish-green skin was crawling from the water. Another look to the trees, and she saw a handful of things Ashling's size, but with moth-like wings, and distinct malice in their eyes, each armed with little knitting-needle-like swords. One more noise drew her eyes to the other side of camp as realization set in: they were surrounded.

Then her eyes settled on a familiar face: the baseball cap, the jagged grin, and the eyes. As the redcap advanced on her, flanked by two others, Megan froze in terror.

Chapter 26: Much Obliged

"We're here to escort you," the redcap in the '49ers hat said, taking a few more steps towards Megan. "To make sure that sword gets where it belongs." Megan couldn't help but notice, now that she was seeing the faerie things for what they really were, that the bat looked a lot more metallic, with numerous spikes along its length.

"You'll forgive me, Peadar, if I don't exactly trust you," Cassia snarled at him, the two cats moving to her side.

"Awww, what's the matter, Cass? Don't like even odds?" he sing-songed back. "Just come along quietly. We're not here to hurt you."

The moth-winged things looked between each other, and the sound of wind whispering through the trees arose again. Megan guessed that they may have either been surprised about the 'not hurting' part, or were amending it to "Yet." Cassia was back-talking without hesitation, but the whole group was injured, and Megan still couldn't move.

Then she heard a whispered song in her ear, hints of a tune. Fixating on the music, she hummed the music Ashling was feeding her, and the fear lessened. She hummed louder, quickly drawing the attention of the creatures around them, and Peadar forgot about Cassia to focus entirely on Megan. This time, with the music reverberating in her mind, she stared right back at him, then stepped forward. This time, it was the redcap who retreated a step.

The hesitation didn't last long. He snarled, raised the weapon, and rushed at her. There was movement to one side and a flash of blue as Peadar swung the spiked club. When Megan's brain caught up with events, Justin was standing between her and Peadar, and the Claiomh Solais had cleaved directly through the redcap's weapon.

The Jenny Greenteeth hissed and started forward, then stopped when Justin turned to point the flaming sword at her. The other redcaps tensed, then backed away on finding Cassia and the cats alike growling at them. The whispering in the wind picked up.

Megan looked towards the group of not-pixies, who seemed to be directing their magics, as far as she could tell. For a moment, they looked intently at Justin and his sword, gesturing towards him, then looked at each other, confused, when their magic seemed to wash over him without effect.

Louder this time, Ashling hummed a different tune in Megan's ear, one recognizable from the music book. Megan picked it up, singing the words this time, and gestured. All three of the moth-winged things were lifted out of their tree branch by a sudden, fierce breeze and carried back into the woods.

"Who sent you?" Cassia asked Peadar as the rest of the Unseelie gang backed away.

"Can't tell you. Sworn to secrecy," he responded, not backing away like the others, but not looking nearly as threatening anymore either.

Megan glanced at the will o' wisp, which was drifting back into the woods. "I have a guess. I suppose you can't tell us where you planned to escort us, either?"

"Couldn't tell you if I wanted to," he replied, standing his ground even as the hag slipped back into the water.

"We don't need an escort, and we know where we're going," She had a brief impulse to tell Justin or Cassia to hit him, to get the point across, before another thought hit, admiring his conviction. She settled on, "Get out of here."

To her surprise, the redcap nodded, reaching down to pick up the other half of his club and backing away. "Sure. We just wanted to make sure you got there safe and sound. Look like you've got a handle on it," Then his grin returned. "No hard feelings?"

Megan's first thought was of her father's words, 'distinctly not idea people.' She nodded back, surprising herself a little at her own choice of words. "No hard feelings." She was more surprised that she felt entirely sincere about it. "But you owe me one."

She was even more surprised at his response, especially in light of what she'd heard about the weight of favors here. Instead of more snarling and posturing, he bowed deeply to her. "You've got it, Highness," He glanced around at the other redcaps and the moth-winged things starting to peek their heads back out. "Come on, you cowardly bastards, let's go."

When Megan looked back around at the others, she noticed Lani, in particular, staring incredulously. "Did that just happen?"

"I'm...actually not sure," Megan responded, a little confused, with more time to process, but suddenly feeling a lot less hurt, and a lot more confident in their mission.

Justin sheathed the sword and moved to Megan's right side. "Thank you. I'm not sure what you did with their magic, but..."

"That wasn't her," Cassia said. "That's one of the things the sword is all about. How do you think those heroes of old Ireland stood up against sorcerers and Fomoire and all sorts of magical this-and-thats? You're not invulnerable—but a few sprite tricks aren't going to slow you down. Oh, and you should see what it does to undead things."

"Undead?" Megan said.

"Don't worry," Cassia said. "I can outrun them."

"That's... actually not very reassuring," Megan told her.

Cassia hooked the cats up to her chariot, now not only working, but scratch-free. "Sure it is. I feel much better." She helped Lani up onto the chariot with her, whether out of thanks for the repairs, or because she still had the worst injuries wasn't clear.

In preparation for the trip, the Count landed on Megan's shoulder, Ashling dismounting and crawling around the back of her neck to sit on Megan's other shoulder. "Besides, no one has seen any undead things in forever. There's some cults with necromantic leanings here and there around the world, but they're probably harmless. And I guess there might be a vampire or two in Washington D.C., but that's just kind of a given, right?" the pixie said.

"You're no help either," Megan replied, before setting off after Cassia and the chariot, with the others close behind.

After a few more miles of travel, Justin turned, heading off the path and deeper into the woodlands.

"The castle is this way." Lani pointed.

"We're not going to the castle," Justin said. "The stone's this way."

Lani and Megan exchanged a glance, then Megan turned to follow. A moment later, Cassia turned the chariot and moved to follow as well.

As they walked, Ashling started muttering. For some time, and a few miles, Megan didn't pay it much mind. Then she heard the strangest thing she'd heard yet from Ashling—at least given what she knew of the pixie. "Huh... I'm not even sure where this is."

Cassia apparently heard her, too. "Well, if we get ambushed again, our hardworking young man can apparently handle things with one hand tied against his side," she said, grinning.

Justin just stared straight ahead. "There it is," he said, heading for a very small clearing. In it was a gray stone, perfectly cylindrical, sitting on the ground.

"Well, Justin, get the sword in the rock so we can get on with the rest of the job," said Megan. "Matters of life and death and all."

As Justin nodded and drew the blade, Ashling suddenly spoke hurriedly, even by Ashling standards. "Megan, I just remembered where this is, and that's not a rock. I've only ever come here with the Unseelie King, and..."

"Ashling, I'm sure it's a great story with a lot of interesting definitions, but let Justin finish his deal first."

And in a flurry of white and blue sparks, Justin stabbed the blade into the stone.

Chapter 27: Flame War

For a moment, nothing happened, and Justin reached for the sword again. Before he could take hold of it, blue flame shot upward from the stone, shooting high into the air. Surprised, Justin staggered back. As the flame lowered, a shockwave rippled out from the stone, the outer edge ringed with blue flame. Megan dove just in time, and even then, the force rolled her backwards. Justin landed next to her, stunned and groaning, but at least still moving. The others ended up scattered around the clearing, with Cassia catching and shielding Lani with her body before they crashed into a tree. Ashling and the Count both went tumbling much further, disappearing back into the woods.

As Megan watched, blue flames licked across the surface of the stone, etching ancient Celtic symbols in the facing surface. Even after the flames passed each symbol, continuing to write something across the stone, the symbols still flickered with occasional sparks or tiny tongues of flame. Megan couldn't make out the writing, but even from where she was, could feel power and heat radiating off of the stone.

"What did that just do?" Megan asked, trying to clear her head while looking around for signs of Ashling.

"Exactly what I needed it to," said a clear-ringing voice. Orlaith, accompanied by her General, a dozen of the sidhe knights, and twice as many brownies, stepped into the clearing from the other side. A host of pixies—Megan couldn't say how many glimmers that was—emerged from the woods, settling into the trees around the edges.

"It will fuel the balefires," the Queen continued. "A constant, dependable energy source will keep them burning, keep the paths clear and safe. We don't need detours for maintenance. We don't need Unseelie tricks to stoke them. We will never need the Unseelie to run anything again. Now that it's obsolete, I am canceling the Dance, this year and forever."

"Canceling the Dance?" Lani was the next to speak. "That's insane. Do you realize what that will do to Earth?"

Orlaith turned her head, glancing at Lani for a few moments before answering. "Earth will survive. As soon as stability is ensured, we'll see what we can do to help mitigate any damage. We must look to the good of Faerie, first."

Cassia was next, half-growling her words as she pulled herself up to stand behind Lani. "You're asking for war. The Unseelie aren't going to stand for this."

"The Unseelie are a nuisance. They are a mess. They are a prison mob that that is allowed to run loose year after year. I am choosing to end the cycle and keep things in the hands of those of us who know what we're doing."

"By shoving a flaming sword into your delicately-balanced system?" Megan interjected.

"I can control it," was Orlaith's slow, almost staccato reply. "It can be controlled."

"But ... but won't there be a huge fight?" Megan asked.

"Here's hoping," said Cassia.

The queen just smiled. "Who knows? There are a few Unseelie who can see reason sometimes," she said with a cryptic lightness. "As for the rest, how would they become informed and organized before Samhain? Even if they did, we have the upper hand until then—and now we always will."

"When my dad went missing in the first place... " Megan began.

"I may have mentioned how very, very impressive an Ellén Trechend would be for the Samhain feast at the ball. I may have mentioned that it was just possible for a sufficiently skilled and dashing hunter to bring in such a trophy from the Winter Marches before the paths even shifted. And then, certain reasonable people may have done what they found necessary."

The words echoed a bit as Megan heard them. Her brain scrambled to the last time she heard a phrase like that, and the wince on her face took on several different aspects. She struggled to listen, her heart pounding with anger, hurt, and confusion, to the Queen's next declaration.

"Justin of Ludlow," Orlaith said. "Our deal is done. You are under no further geasa."

"Guess what?" Megan asked automatically, little though she was in the mood for another vocabulary lesson. Ashling still didn't pop up to give one, anyway.

"She doesn't have any other jobs for me before I go home," Justin, still bowing slightly, explained in the careful tone of a boy who realizes he's pleased some very dangerous people and accidentally upset others.

"Exactly," Orlaith said. "Ludlow is still lovely this time of year, crumbling castle walls and all. Admittedly, right now that particular path would be especially..." She glanced at the sword and the blue-sparking conduit. "...hot. Uncomfortably so."

"So we'll all be waiting comfortably together at the castle," Cassia asked, sneering. "With this nice comfortable escort and maybe a comfortable cell—or a comfortable pyre?"

"I don't think there'd be any point to that. I can send some pixies with you temporarily—"

"They already have one, thank you, Majesty." Ashling's voice was cold as the Count finally flew out of the trees. "Come on," she said, and all the Queen's pixies and all the Queen's men made no move as Ashling led the girls, the chariot, and Justin out of the clearing.

"I told you it wasn't a rock," Ashling said.

"You also told me you evolved from baby's laughter and that he's called the Count because he has a widow's peak!" Megan replied. "Anyway, I..." There was too much. Just too much. So she seized on one thing she thought she could address. "I kind of have a feeling who might have helped with all this by arranging the Unseelie involved in the ambush."

"The Gray Lady?"

"Ah. Yeah. So...is that why you were mad at her when we met her?" Megan had wondered, but there'd always been too many other questions.

"Sort of. I didn't know anything, but she's been on his case for years. A few nagging whispers about his travels and all. And—"

"She's into will o' wisps."

"Yeah. I'm going to give her such a piece of my mind after I've taken you home."

Megan paused for a moment. "You're talking to Justin, right?"

"No," Ashling said. "Easier to just bring him to Seattle, too. He'll deal."

Justin, walking along with an ornate empty sheath at his side, wisely made no objection.

"Oh, then we've got a problem," Megan said after a pause. "I don't know that I want to go home anytime soon."

Chapter 28: Over Lunch

The trip back to An Teach Deiridh, after Ashling stared at Megan for a moment, then changed course, was made in uncomfortable silence, with no one sure how best to address the situation—or willing to risk other pixies, sprites, or will o' wisps listening in. This might well have been the only thing that held Lani back as she looked intently at Megan throughout the walk. Despite the obvious discomfort amongst the group, they stuck together.

Cassia did not unhitch the cats from the chariot. Instead, she drove it directly into the front atrium. A brownie scurried up to them. "We prefer no vehicles inside," she—definitely she; Megan could tell—said with a big nervous smile at the satyress.

Cassia glared, and the brownie started to retreat under her gaze, but Megan stepped in between them before Cassia said a word. "Can you please see that food is delivered to my father's room?"

"To your... father's room? Yes, yes, of course, Highness," the little faerie agreed, almost stumbling over her feet trying to get some distance. She did not try again to stop Cassia from just driving in, and neither did Megan. The wheels occasionally made a clacking sound against the smooth stone floor, but not enough to drown out the Click-Click-Click sound the cats' claws made.

"To your father's room? Why are we going there?" Lani asked as they all headed right into the Unseelie wing. The wheels on the floors soon went more Rumble-Rumble-Rumble as the stone texture shifted. There were still crowds in the halls, but everyone got out of Cassia's way.

"Well, for one thing, we're going to eat. Here's hoping with dessert, too." Megan sniffed the air. "Like that apple cobbler somebody's baking. That'd hit the spot."

"We don't need anything from any of the Queen's ass-kissers," Cassia snarled. "I should start gathering the mob."

"Then don't eat," Megan said, "But stay with us a while before you do anything. You heard her, and Ashling. She has allies all over. Do you really trust all the people in your mob?"

Cassia, shaking her head and muttering, directed the cats forward, past Riocard's chambers. Maxwell strode on, snarling. Jude, however, attempted to turn towards Megan.

Cassia halted the now-skidding chariot before it fell over. She looked at Jude, who now sat beside Megan in his aviator helmet. The helmet was the color of rich coffee with cream that smelled like aged leather and...strawberries? Megan could only guess that maybe Jude had gotten into something requiring Cassia (or more likely, Cassia's girlfriend) to give the poor kitty a bath with whatever shampoo was handy.

"Seriously?" Cassia said, staring at him.

The leopard growled something in response.

"Okay, okay. So we couldn't trust most of them before all of this," Cassia agreed out loud, "You're still being a traitor."

The cat didn't move.

"Okay, fine. You have a plan. Let's go. But no lunch. Her Anal-Retentiveness would probably have us poisoned."

"If she wanted us dead, she'd have killed us. No one would have known," Lani said.

"She might want us dead," Megan said as she mimicked Ashling's previous words to open the door, then got them all safely in. Even the Count decided to perch above the inner doorframe this time. "But she definitely wants something else more. I figured that much out."

"Wait, what?" Lani said as the door closed.

"My Dad was able to talk to me, back near the city," Megan said as she casually lifted a hand to offer Ashling a path from the perch to her shoulder. It was accepted. "She imprisoned him. She didn't kill him. She expects him back someday, even if she hopes it's way after she's totally secured her super-rule and all. When he does, she knows after all he went through to protect me, having actually directly hurt me would mean she wouldn't be able to manipulate him into some kind of settlement. So we're a peace offering."

"Okay, agreed," said Lani. "She's not going to try anything to hurt us. What's this about not going back? This place is still dangerous."

"Of course it is. But I get it. I have a lot to learn...but I sort of want to. My dad will be back someday. I can order a staff around. The guy who tried to kill me with a baseball bat owes me a favor. And I know magic. This place makes sense. Home doesn't."

Lani gave her a quizzical glance. "Say all of that again, and see if it still makes sense to you. Including the part about people trying to kill you with baseball bats. Especially that part."

"Okay, so that still sucked," Megan said. "But look what I have to go back to. Either take just enough pills to struggle through every schoolday, or take them all and be a zombie. Besides, isn't Earth kind of about to start sucking a lot more? How bad is that going to get, anyway?"

"Well, it's hard to say, especially now that she's using the sword like some kind of… 'clean coal.' It'll help, sure. Stoking the fires up will keep the worst of the path-problems from hurting Faerie and Earth both any time too soon. But just because we won't have abominable snowmen in the Bermuda Triangle by Christmas doesn't mean we're okay. The thing is, both courts need to rule. Our side brings the light and the structure to keep everything from being lost like some kind of hurricane."

Megan nodded. "And what does our side bring?" The words came easy, so very easy.

"Y—the Unseelie bring the unrestrained passion. 'Hot blood on cold winter nights' and stuff like that. I have no idea what they do to clear paths and burn fires and drive off the worst of the cold. They don't exactly publish a manual. But I know some of it's creepy."

"The balefires are at least stoked, though."

"Yeah, but that's the kicker. Even supposing the sword really will provide an unlimited stable fuel source—and she didn't present a lot of data—there's the other problem for Earth. Evenly-stoked fire is for sitting around to tell old stories, and that's good. But it only gets you old stories. The first thing that's going to happen on Earth is that there will be no new horror. No new creepy books published. No new slasher films—well, maybe sequels for a while, but that's it."

"Not exactly a nightmare scenario. More like a lack-of-nightmare scenario," Megan said, but something in her felt funny all the same. "There's more to it than that, isn't there?"

"Yeah, that's just the first sign. The cold will keep creeping in, a dry, sterile cold. The paralysis'll get everywhere in the creative industries. Writers and filmmakers of every genre. Musicians—well, not every musician whose spark dies out can get an admin job. Possibly more Christmas shopping, but fewer Christmas pageants. It won't stop with what we think of as the arts, either. There's lots of passions to chill, sparks that can go out. Without the Dance, fewer gardeners will prep their gardens for the next phase. This hunting season will see hunters shrug, save time, and buy a few packs of sausage at the grocery store. All kinds of human reflections of autumn and winter change will happen less, which means spring will actually bring less renewal and rebirth. If it goes on long enough, it'll start to reflect in the seasons themselves."

"Okay, that is bad. But what can we do?"

"I'll talk to my parents. There's other faeries out there. Just because she has some Unseelie allies doesn't mean all the Seelie will agree with her. We need to go back, though."

"What about Justin?

Lani looked to him in turn. "Do you want to wait for a path to clear to England?"

"No, I'll go to Seattle. I don't know anyone else. And more importantly, just because she won't kill you doesn't mean no one will try. The Unseelie are just as likely to come after you, hoping to rile up their King later. I would help protect you, if I might be allowed? Better than starving in streets where I only recognize the ruins."

As he spoke, Megan listened, but casually walked back to the door. She was just reaching it when there was a knock. She opened the door to the brownie, who was balancing two trays of food and a pitcher of lemonade. "Thank you." she said, taking the pitcher, letting the brownie trail her in with the trays. "Brownies, timing. Let's not starve," she said, by way of explanation. "Especially with a long walk this afternoon."

"So, are you coming back to Earth?" Lani asked.

"I hope we all are, because I'm pretty sure I'm going to need help. I have to get my dad out before Halloween. You can check with your parents and anyone else. I'll go back for now...but it's only for now. We're going to come back and save my dad and fix this," she paused, looking a little less determined and more sheepish. "I just don't know how yet."

Chapter 29: Heading Home

"I can't believe she set my dad up for an ambush with peer pressure." Megan sat on Cassia's couch, exhausted from the return to what she had difficulty calling normality.

"That wasn't peer pressure," Cassia said, stopping her pacing around her apartment for a moment. "That was flirting. Like I said, Riocard has a type."

Megan had to admit that, in a very distant way, her mother and the Queen could be said to look a little bit alike.

"Obviously, the Seelie Queen and the Unseelie King are never, ever going to be an actual item," Cassia continued. "Which just makes the flirting worse."

"The flirting isn't what matters," Lani insisted. "Her terrible, terrible plan is what matters."

"Now, Lani, it's totally understandable to be upset that things went so...unexpectedly," Kerr piped up soothingly, having been called over as soon as they were back. "But it's the Queen. She knows a lot more than we do. I really don't think she would go with an actually terrible plan."

"Pretty sure pissing me off this much was a terrible plan," Cassia said. "I'm still waiting for the part where there's a plan to go back, get the sword, and find somewhere else to stick it."

Kerr flushed. Lani answered. "She's not going to let us get the sword back, even if we could. There's the whole fire thing." Justin looked like he was about to respond, but quieted when she continued. "And knights and pixies. She'll have it under guard."

"I don't have a plan yet anyway," Megan said. "I will, or, more likely, Lani and Justin will come up with something with all of you. There's a lot more of you here to discuss it. I need to go home soon. I still have a couple of tests coming up. You're sure my mother didn't suspect anything?" she asked Kerr.

"No, no, nothing, Highness. All of your homework was turned in on time. Everything went smoothly. The math test is next Thursday. Your mother is working a little late tonight."

"So, can we keep at the homework help thing?" Megan was hopeful.

Kerr shuffled from tiny foot to tiny foot. "Well, um, technically, Highness..."

Lani sighed. "Megan, please don't abuse a carefully worded two-century-old diplomatic agreement between supernatural communities to get a B+ in chemistry."

"I had to try," Megan said. "Besides, technically, my job in Faerie isn't done yet, right?"

"Come up with a plan, and then we can talk about using faerie magic to cheat on your next math test. Meanwhile, you're going back on your pills, right? But not all of them."

"The multi-colored pills, spread out a bit when Mom's not looking, and Vitamin C supplements," Megan agreed. "Things started making more sense without them in Faerie, but I don't know when we're going back."

"I'll be there to make sure she gets her Vitamin C," Ashling piped in helpfully.

Megan started to sigh, then stopped and looked at Ashling intently. "How long have you been there?" she asked. "Right on the edge of the corner of my eye?"

"Hey, I've been flattered by how long you've had a thing for butterflies."

"Heh. Yeah. Well, you're welcome. Or thank you, or something." She looked to Lani and Justin. "Well, anyway, we'll go back when we know what to do."

"We'll be ready," Justin said.

"Good. Um...where will you be ready?" The second-most obvious thing to Megan was that she wasn't going to leave Justin to fend for himself in Seattle. The most obvious thing was that she couldn't take him home.

"I can give our hardworking boy a place here, for a three-day trial run at least," Cassia said, looking him up and down.

Justin twitched at the suggestion. Cassia saw it and smirked. Lani saw it and stepped up. "He'll stay with us. Mom will insist," she said. And Mrs. Kahale might well insist once Lani told her she needed to insist about something. "We'll talk to the right people about getting him an ID and stuff."

"They can do that?" Megan asked.

Kerr shuffled. Once again, Lani filled in the details. "Faeries can do a lot of things, depending on the faerie. I understand that it took them a while to adapt to needing to forge driver's licenses and passports and things when they used to be able to just show up. Some of them quit bothering. Some of them adapted."

"Forging documents, and here I was feeling a little guilty about having a brownie doing my homework."

"Yes, and some of them also hunt and eat people, or bludgeon travelers to make hat dyes. So, you know, not necessarily the best role models."

"Hey, you're half-faerie too."

"Yes, half the type of faerie who feel very, very guilty when we don't get the extra wing of the temple finished in one night."

"Guilt is highly overrated," Cassia said.

Megan grinned. "Work schedules and owls. You Hawaiian lawn gnome people are very strange."

Lani rolled her eyes, doing her best not to smile through feigned indignation. "Fine, next time build your own bridge."

"As soon as I figure out bridge-building magic, maybe I will."

"That's pretty unlikely to be one of your tricks," Ashling said.

"I thought you didn't know this magic?"

"I don't, but I knew plenty of people who did, and heard about more of them. Annie the Fair, Tom O'Shaughnessy, "Magic" Roger Barr, Heather Riordan, Moon Unit Zappa..."

"Wait, Moon Unit knows bardic magic?"

"No, I just really like her name. Where was I going with that?"

"You were telling me why I can't build bridges."

"Oh, right. You see, all of the world's magic comes from a pact with the first dragons. They didn't look anything like dragons you hear about now, though. Back then, though of course they had the same intellectual rigor that made one dragon I know live under a Jesuit university, they—"

"Does this have anything to do with bridges?" Now Megan was having to force herself not to smile.

"Everything. Dragons grew wings because the bridges wouldn't hold them when they got too big."

"Of course they did."

"True story. But anyway, magic tends to come in themes. Your father has a lot of tricks, but he's really, really good at ice and cold and stuff. One of the best ever. Most of the bard types, whatever else they could do, could do a little healing, and then there's the inspiring the troops things. That's pretty universal. Or it was. Now, instead of music, they have R. Lee Ermey, but the point stands. Anyway, you're still going to have a specialty for bigger things. And some songs just won't work for you."

"How will I know?"

"Well, if you sing along to something, and nothing happens, then that song doesn't work for you."

Megan was about to respond, but noticed Lani and Kerr giggling, causing her to pause before finally answering, "Okay, that's obvious. How will I know what I'm going to be good at?"

"See what feels natural."

"Really, that's it?"

Ashling grinned wide. "You were expecting something different?"

"Well, yes, actually. Magic seems like a pretty big deal. You would think there would be stuff to study and formulas and...well, math problems. I guess."

"You can use magic, at least partly, because of your faerie side. If you had to focus too much, or do too much math, you couldn't do it."

"Hey, I'm good at math," Lani and Kerr said in near-unison.

Megan glanced at them, then back at Ashling. "All right. I'll bring the book, and you can help me. One more thing to be studying. Speaking of which, I should get home."

Lani stepped up to give her a hug. "We'll think of something, Megan. I promise. We have a week. We're not going to give up."

"I'm definitely not giving up," Megan assured her. "But first, I need to make sure I'm home on time. I'll have a lot harder time saving the world if I'm grounded."

Chapter 30: Family Dinner

Megan paced around the house for a while. No brilliant ideas jumped out from the corners at her, so she stopped in the living room again. She went to look at the photo albums, to see her dad again, then paused, wondering if her mother had anything else left over from that other era.

She went into her mother's room and through the closet, finding her mother's old bass guitar tucked into the far back corner. As she was about to take it out for closer examination, she noticed a couple of old cardboard boxes on the high shelf at the back of the closet, gathering dust.

Megan fetched a chair, climbed, and dragged the boxes down. One was full of Christmas decorations that she'd never seen in use. The lights were all neatly coiled, and the holly, mistletoe, and ornaments were neatly separated and stacked. This was true to her mother's usual style, but they were all definitely decorations. She wondered how long it had been since they'd been put up. From the amount of them, she was pretty sure there was plenty for both a tree, and to put a few lights along the edge of the roof.

The other box was even more interesting. The more fragile contents of the box were protected by a handful of neatly folded 'Late to the Party' T-shirts, with tour dates along the West Coast on the back. Everything else in the box was equally neatly laid out and organized to make the best use of the space. Drumsticks, packs of guitar strings, extra guitar picks, two guitar maintenance kits— Megan somehow wasn't surprised her mother had spare items and repair kits for all sorts of emergencies.

What really caught her attention, though, were the CDs. There were almost a dozen in all, counting the ones showing as singles and a studio demo, in addition to the three full albums. She picked up the one on the top. The black cover bore a picture of an overturned red plastic cup and white letters reading '*Late to the Party: It Actually Is 1999.*' Surprisingly in Megan's experience of such things, at least with her own computer software, the CD inside actually was the album labeled on the case.

Since the box obviously hadn't been disturbed in ages, she figured the CD wouldn't be missed. She returned everything in both boxes to their proper places and order, then put the boxes back. Then she took the CD to her room and put it into the player.

According to the liner notes, the first song was called "Complications." The song opened on drums, steady as a heartbeat. Within moments, a few lines of bass were added, then silenced to let the heartbeat take center stage again, picking back up now and then, only to fade back to the drums. Twenty seconds in, Megan was a bit startled by a guitar wail, set against the steady background. The wail trailed off, and a slightly discordant, minor-key guitar line took its place. A few moments later the singing began. *"Three months in my nightgown / after three of puke and sweat..."*

It wasn't exactly high poetry, but Megan was transfixed. The voice was raw. Oh, it was tired. If it hadn't been, Megan might not have recognized her mother's voice at all. But under and around the weariness in the performance was an energy that was almost electrifying.

It took a moment, as the young Sheila O'Reilly melodically howled through a litany of physical, mental, and emotional horrors, for Megan to process what the song was about. She'd written it while pregnant. *"So I'm crying into pillows, / and I'm screaming on your shoulder / and I know I had my options, / But I want to see you hold her."*

Megan turned off the player for a while.

When her mother got home, Megan had supper ready. Kerr had done most of it, of course. Fortunately, it was pancakes and omelets, so Megan wouldn't have to explain why she was suddenly a gourmet chef. She wouldn't be asked to repeat anything impossible, either. Of course, standing there putting pancakes onto plates felt bizarre after everything that had happened — and everything at risk of happening. Still, why not?

Her mother's smile was thin and tired, but it was there. "Thanks so much, sweetie," she said with a quick kiss to Megan's forehead.

They settled in at the table. "How's school?"

"School's good." *A nice faerie person filled in for me there while I was trying to save the monster-king who wore out that other you who liked music, the you I never got to know. But I couldn't save him, so now all the faeries might be like mystic-dinosaurs arguing whether the mystic-meteor is coming. I'm not even sure what regular people are in this analogy, but there'll be fewer movies.* "My math project got an A. That should help balance things out if I have trouble on the tests again."

"Oh, that's wonderful! I'm proud of you. And I'm so glad we finally have something that really fixes things. Might fix your trouble with math tests, too."

"Maybe." Or the orange pills might have made her write the same equation 27 times each for the first two questions and not answer anything else. Lani's having been right that there was a problem there wasn't very reassuring in terms of hoping she was wrong about Orlaith's attempt to Fix the Whole Thing.

Sheila O'Reilly, however, was just nodding and looking wistfully at the bottle from which she was removing a large lime green pill to take with her meal. Those had been at every supper for as long as Megan could remember. She now wondered if they worked better for someone whose depression wasn't magically induced.

"Hey, Mom," she said, pulling her mother's attention away from the pills. "Next week, can I study at Lani's for the big test on Thursday?"

"As long as you make sure you're focused on studying and not painting plates again, then of course."

Megan offered no argument about the occasional pottery projects of the past. "Okay, thanks. Then after the test, if I'm feeling pretty good about it and caught up on my other homework, can I go out and do Halloween things with the Kahales? Maybe even spend the whole weekend?" Because as handy as Kerr had been, she didn't want to make the brownie have to miss the Dance, nor did Megan want to risk having to sneak out.

"You'll get all of your homework done first? And you're not going to stay out too late? There's a lot of strange people out that night."

Her mother didn't know the half of it, and Megan certainly wasn't going to tell her. More importantly, the answer hadn't been 'No,' even if it came with conditions. "I think her little brother wants to go trick-or-treating. We'll be indoors before it gets too dark, though." The ballroom was indoors, after all.

"All right, I know you've been working hard. We'll see how you're feeling after the test. If you're all caught up, I suppose a sleepover is reasonable. The Kahales know you'll be there?"

"Yes, Mom." That, at least, was true. She was more than a little envious of Lani being able to be so open with her parents. At least it meant there would be so-called responsible adults to cover for them when they carried out the plan. Not that she had a plan yet, but there was no way she was missing the Dance.

Chapter 31: Back to School

Megan almost wished the week would go by in a haze, but going back to her old dosage failed to produce one. After a day or two of the multicolored pills, she was in a middling ground: concentration was sometimes a struggle, and she still saw Ashling often out of the corner of her eye, but she felt... functionally human. Work could be done. She would study alongside Lani on the bus, then exchange anxious glances, as neither of them still had any real plan.

School happened. The margins of her composition books got more varied, occasionally with thorn-vines and highlighter-yellow eyes. In art class, Mrs. Chang looked at Megan's in-class work—a pastel sketch of moths and butterflies dueling with knitting needles—and was more pleased than Megan had seen her in weeks.

At home, she had another butterfly picture pinned above her desk, the one covered in conic-section equations and a large red 'A' with a note of "Interesting presentation!" Even if it had been triple-checked and turned in by a brownie, she still felt proud, and that helped her feel confident as she reviewed the process.

Math, chemistry, and art weren't her only renewed focuses of work. The music teacher, Ms. Dahl, found herself beset with a lot more questions than usual. Megan's questions on the history of music theory seemed to come out of nowhere. Megan was grateful that at least her accounts of ancient and medieval musical terms balanced out Ashling's random etymologies.

Sometimes the pixie's accounts made sense. Sometimes they made too much sense. Sometimes they weren't helpful at all. And sometimes Megan was pretty sure they weren't involved in the same conversation. Despite all of it, she had been learning, and learning quickly. She had no idea why particular songs, whether from the songbook or internet radio stations, worked to do what they did. Some songs very much matched up with certain effects in pace and feel; some seemed almost opposite.

A few of the songs in the book didn't seem to do anything at all, which Ashling mostly wrote off as not being Megan's 'thing.' She couldn't tell if the healing magic was any more effective or not, since she wasn't quite willing to injure herself to test it over the week, despite Ashling's urging, but she still felt better when she used it. Inspirational songs had been easier, other than the times Megan's mother had had to visit to tell her to keep it down. She quickly found out that those worked better the louder they were sung.

Most interesting to Megan, in part because they came the easiest, were the winds. With a few different songs, both old ones from the books, and some personal favorites she experimented with, she was able to direct gusts of wind. With practice came finesse.

The majority of academic studying took place at Lani's. Between bouts of chemistry homework and algebra notes, Mrs. Kahale occasionally found it necessary to give Megan a hug.

Justin was there, both an issue and not an issue at all. The Kahales had welcomed him with open arms. He was soon installed, sharing the hastily-but-sturdily-built bunk bed in Mack's room. Mack was not nearly as put out by this imposition as Justin was confused by the fact that the five-year-old had previously had his own room. Justin was understandably confused by a lot of things. He and Mack went to bed at the same time each night, as Justin was unused to staying up late.

School was not yet a possibility for Justin; paperwork was being secured, but he was obviously foreign, and the appropriate channels for exchange students in the school system would take a while. Which was just as well. It would take a lot to make Justin remotely ready to tackle high school. So while the Kahales were all either in class or at work, Justin had apparently been sitting around the house trying to absorb information. Whenever Megan and Lani had study sessions, Justin would sit with them and listen intently, but obviously unable to contribute—or really comprehend much.

Cassia wasn't around much during the study sessions. She'd tried to brainstorm with Lani, Justin, and Ashling the initial weekend, but according to Lani, was too champing at the bit to think of any good ideas.

Ashling's ideas were all over the board, but tended to veer off in an angry direction as well. When not trying to insert snippets of bardic advice into chemistry homework, she had some strong theories as to why the Gray Lady may have been so 'reasonable' to Orlaith's plans. Perhaps the seneschal had gotten too used to running all things Unseelie and resented the King. Perhaps the queen had promised her something. Perhaps the bean sidhe's grief had fueled jealousy, since even after leaving his human family behind, Riocard still had a daughter out there. Still, the pixie had no concrete thoughts about what to do.

Megan's mind jumped around too, though not to pixielike degrees. She knew now that they couldn't simply wait Orlaith's coup out. But whenever she and Lani seemed to be making small amounts of progress after schoolwork was done, it was always time to get home for the evening. Ashling would follow her home and pick up on the magic advice. The evenings had turned out best for this. At the points her medication was at its best effect, she had more trouble with her magic.

After a little practice, she started to see Ashling's point regarding study and concentration. It really was coming easier when she just went with what felt right—and the more fully she let herself get into the music, the better. Likewise, concentrating too much, or trying to work out the exact whys something did or didn't work seemed to make everything come harder. Her best results came just before her mother got home or in the brief times before her mother came to tell her to turn down the music or tone down the singing. A few times, she wondered what she might be able to do if she left off the pills entirely again. The combination of the test and their lack of a plan stopped her... for now.

On Thursday, the math test came. Megan had done the job studying; she understood the concepts. She just had to make sure to stay focused enough to not screw up the problems. When it was over, she felt she would get by. She celebrated in a dance of whirling leaves behind the house that night. It was a little incongruous, having Ashling being the one to tell her she had to be careful, mid-dance, but she supposed she couldn't have her mother thinking treatment wasn't working.

Chapter 32: Pre-Halloween

When Megan walked in Friday after school, the traditional Kahale Pre-Halloween was already underway: Mack had halfway completed a hard hat made entirely out of LEGOs.

Justin sat on the bed in some of Mrs. Kahale's gardening clothes. They and some hand-me-downs from Cassia made up his entire modern wardrobe so far. Megan could see why he preferred the gardening clothes to the 'Let's Do Something Wrong' T-Shirt. The chain mail was in the closet, and the sheath of the Sword of Light was hung neatly on one of Mack's brightly-colored plastic coat-hooks. Thankfully, when they went back, he'd be able to wear the chain mail.

She gave Lani a brief hug, then sat down next to Justin and let Lani get back to work on her Firefly-inspired spaceship mechanic costume. Megan was well aware that the costume pieces Lani hadn't been able to find second-hand had been hand stitched over the course of the week. Her red cape and picnic basket were feeling a little inadequate, but she'd had other channels for her artistic leanings this week. Megan didn't do nearly so much with so little time as Lani did. "How are you adjusting?" she finally asked Justin.

"Well enough. They've been trying to get me ready for school, but I'm uncertain how quickly that will proceed. There's no lack of things to do, though. Especially while we try to save as much of the final crop as possible."

"Final crop? So you've been introduced to the pumpkin mausoleum?"

He grinned at the designation for Mrs. Kahale's garden. "There are some survivors. I think the radishes may be a lost cause, though. Perhaps they would be best left in their graves."

"Not for lack of effort."

"Certainly not. She puts in plenty of time. I'm just not quite certain how to tell her that she's a terrible gardener."

"I think she'd be the first to agree with you," Lani said, taking a break in her preparations, "It doesn't really matter. That's not the point. It relaxes her, gives her something to do when not at work, and, well, we eat the survivors, so there's no witnesses."

Megan laughed. "So what's it going to be this year when it gets too cold to salvage anything else from the killing fields?"

"I don't know yet. She's mentioned poetry. She might try to spend more time battling the spinning wheel. Or maybe the pottery wheel. Or getting the two confused and making a mess."

Justin looked back and forth between them quizzically.

"Have you been down into the basement?"

"With the wheel and full furnace and all?" he asked.

"Ah, good. So you did find the island of misfit vases. Two of those are from when Lani and I were really little. The others... yeah, that's Mrs. K."

"I'm not sure I understand. She seems so happy with these things, but they all turn out so badly?"

Lani grinned. "She's exceedingly happy to be gardening, or playing with her pottery wheel, or baking... fortunately, the 14th Century seems to have produced iron stomachs."

"Chocolate... is weird," Justin said simply.

"By most people's standards, you still haven't eaten chocolate yet. But anyway, enjoying her collection is the whole point. Mom works hard. She's a very good office manager. It's a nice, boring break away from living with a faerie and two half-faeries. When she gets home, she can indulge in something fun, and no one, most especially herself, cares if she's any good at it."

"Collection?" Justin asked. "There's collected sickly plants and collected malformed pottery..."

"And you haven't seen her photography or heard her poetry. You weren't around when she accidentally shaped the rock garden into an obscene gesture. Mom collects hobbies."

Justin still looked confused, but nodded his agreement. "I will do what I can to help save some of the gardening victims, then."

"We'll all be glad for the help. I couldn't help but notice you seemed to know your way around growing things in general."

"I helped some with that at home, yes. Along with a lot of whatever else was needed. Tending the dogs and horses, cleaning boots and armor, maintaining weapons, and general repairs. Though I will admit, your house is definitely not in need of any general repairs."

"Lack of dogs and horses too. Don't mention those to Mack. Mom only recently convinced him that cowboy-telephone-line-repairman as a costume might be a little too complex for most people to recognize what he was. Thank goodness for LEGOs."

"And you're getting dressed up even though we're going to the Dance instead of out to a party or something?" Megan asked Lani.

"It doesn't matter what costume I wore, I'd still stand out a lot less than most things at the Dance. And I enjoy it. I still think Justin's knight costume ought to win most accurate, though."

"I'm not a knight yet," Justin replied, "and may never be. I'm definitely taking the armor back to Faerie, though."

"I'm guessing the Kahales were able to patch it up and replace the shield?"

Lani looked at Megan like she was crazy. "Patch? We upgraded it. And his new shield is lighter and twice as durable." Justin nodded his agreement.

"Hey, even better. I'm just glad the armor did its job before. Some of those fights could have been a lot worse."

Justin rolled his recently dislocated shoulder, as if to make sure it worked properly after the injuries. Thankfully, between time and the bits of Megan's healing, it seemed to be almost fully recovered. "I think they were bad enough."

"We'll try for less bad this time, yeah. No more golems and no more explosions." Megan wished she could promise more than that, but it was a good place to start.

"The last I can't promise. I put the sword in the stone. I should try to recover it for you."

"That didn't exactly go well last time. So glad you didn't end up with third-degree burns from the fire or something."

Justin shrugged. "It didn't hurt."

"Oh. Well, yeah, Faerie's weird sometimes about what doesn't hurt." Megan remembered the thorn-vine that had scratched and the briarmail that hadn't.

Lani glanced at the sword sheath. "Sometimes. Or there may just be something about the sword and its sheath that protects the bearer. That is pretty intense flame close up."

"Okay, so maybe there's something to that. It's an awfully big risk, though. It's going to be guarded, even if you can stand the fire."

That part, no one had an answer for. The idea was good, but Megan couldn't think of any way to deal with whoever Orlaith had on watch, and despite the week to talk, the others hadn't come up with anything.

"The Count says that haunted-house grapes don't taste anything remotely like eyeballs," Ashling said, instead of hello, as they landed on the windowsill.

Megan didn't bother to ask where any of that line of comparison came from. From the moment she went to the window to greet them, she was far too captivated by the appearance of Halloween. With the light starting to dim, what lights there were became more obvious, the fog machine of the people next door was turned on, and the clashing decorations all over the neighborhood were somehow just perfect. The mix of ghostly noises, canned screams, and maniacal laughter audible now that the window was open didn't hurt either. She was sure it was just going to be even louder and more perfect tomorrow.

Her reverie was only broken when Lani put a hand on her shoulder. "So, you haven't gotten into your bag yet. What are you going as this year?"

"Eh, I brought my Red Riding Hood cape from last year."

"But you're usually so into dressing up."

"Sure, but there didn't seem to be a lot of point this year. I'm not sure I want any of the candy they'd hand out in Faerie."

"This is the perfect time to dress up," Ashling chimed in.

"I kind of have to agree with her," Lani said. "Weird as that sounds. We could use a little distraction. And this isn't really like you."

Megan blinked, mind going back through some of her old costumes—all homemade, since she was small, and often as much art project as disguise. There was something that felt right about the comment. She just wasn't placing it. "Maybe. I'll have to think about it," She draped the red cape over her shoulders and secured it, pulling the hood up while she pondered. Then, glancing down at the things she'd brought, she dug into the bag again. "But I kind of want to think to music."

Chapter 33: Inspiration

"That's one of your Mom's albums?"

"Yeah... have you heard it before? Cassia apparently has."

"Cassia was a grown woman obsessed with the local music scene before we were born. No, I've never seen it. Mom apparently spent the '90s into five kinds of folk music. That's when she added the ukulele to the collection."

"Figures. Well, I'm all for not being the last one to know what my mom used to sound like. Do you mind?" Since no one minded, Megan put the CD in—but skipped the first track. She hadn't heard the rest, but was pretty sure, from the titles, none of the others had much to do with describing pregnancy complications in way too much detail.

The next song started out a lot differently. Instead of the brooding, heavy guitars in minor key behind the off-kilter poetry, this one opened into a walking baseline. It was like something out of the blues, providing a structure everything else built on as the drums kicked in, then the lead guitar. The lyrics started out almost spoken-word, her mother's voice coming across as intense, but steady and controlled. Megan glanced at the back of the CD. The second track was 'Good Fences (Make Me Crazy).' As she did, the refrain hit, and the song went into full-voiced rock, except for that baseline. Nice and steady, a good fence for all the rock craziness and suddenly melodic screaming.

When the song finally wound to a close, Lani was just staring at the speakers. "Wow... your mother had some kind of voice. That was amazing. What's next?"

Megan glanced at the case again. "Next one, uhm, 'Monster. Peace. Theater.'" She took the words slow, enunciating each as they were written. Yet again, everything shifted. The instrumentals weaved in and out, as her mother sang about late nineties international events. Megan didn't follow all of the references, and some of the lyrics may have not been intended as entirely literal.

Regardless, no one was in any hurry to stop the music, and Megan felt she was meeting whole new sides to her mother with each song.

It got even more personal when she first heard her mother and father interacting. The next song was 'Psych Ward Composition,' with her mother singing the lead. While she sang, the bass was steady, just picking up bit by bit as the song went on. Then, her father took every other verse, providing the rich, dark voices in the head of the fictive 'I' of the song—or perhaps not so fictive. He remained smooth, sounding entirely reasonable despite increasingly erratic suggestions, while the lead's vocals and the accompanying bassline became more and more strained. Only Ashling seemed unperturbed by the song, just swaying and occasionally dancing along to the tune, especially Riocard's parts.

Now, both Megan and Lani were staring at the speakers, a bit wide-eyed. As the song wound down, they exchanged a glance.

"That was intense," Lani offered, pausing the music.

"That might have been the creepiest duet ever," Megan agreed. "They were really, really good. I think this next song might be a little... uhm, lighter, though."

"What's this one?"

Megan showed her the back cover. "'Yet Another Song About Jumping.'"

"That sounds promising. Like something you can dance to, finally," Lani agreed, Ashling notwithstanding. She turned the music back on.

The next song was more or less what it advertised. Amidst making fun of a lot of light, fluffy pop music in a tongue-in-cheek fashion, the song turned out to be not just danceable, but enthusiastically so. Halfway through the song, Megan grabbed for Justin's hand—he had been sitting quietly confused throughout the process of listening to what he had to simply trust was music—and pulled him into the bouncing and jumping around. It took a little bit, but by the time the long song was winding down, he seemed much more relaxed, and even seemed to be enjoying jumping around and dancing with the girls.

If anything, Ashling was even more enthusiastic, hitching a ride from the Count to the top of the speakers so she wouldn't be underfoot while the humans were jumping, then throwing herself into the dance with total abandon—almost falling off several times—while the Count just watched with as bemused an expression as a beak allowed for.

As she danced and let herself relax, more and more of the commentary through the day started to play through Megan's mind. The more she let go of the tension of the week, the more readily ideas came. Nothing was concrete yet, but a plan began to form.

The Jumping song trailed off, then the band opened into "Why Is It Monday?" What struck Megan was how much trouble she had picturing her mother having ever gotten up to the wild weekends that made waking up and going back to normal life so difficult in the song's lament. Listening to what the song expressed as horrors, she was pretty sure her early-twenties mother wouldn't like her current self very much. Of course, thinking of the green pills, Megan admitted it was hard to say whether her mother currently did like herself much.

At the same time, she could hear shades of the same person and personality in the lyrics. She opened up the case, checking through the credits. She somehow wasn't surprised to see her mother's name listed repeatedly. She wrote or helped write almost every song. She played the bass. She sang. She did the cover art photos. She did a lot of the arrangement and sound engineering. Megan considered that, along with the lyrics and what she knew of some of her mother's old contacts. It seemed that even in the days her mother partied hard enough to catch the attention of a faerie king, she was still a hard worker. It was just that, along the way, the partying had disappeared.

When the song ended, she borrowed the remote from Lani, pausing, and then shifting backwards.

"There's still half of the album to go. This is really, really good stuff," Lani protested, but didn't try to stop her.

"I know. We can listen to all of it. I just wanted to hear the Jumping song again. There's just something on the tip of my brain, and jumping helps."

Lani looked confused, Justin looked even more confused. But Ashling was grinning. "That's my girl," the pixie cheered, starting into the dancing before the music even began.

And so the tone shifted again, moving away from the workday lament, and back into playfully making fun of fluffy pop music and encouraging jumping and bouncing around. Megan didn't hesitate this time, grabbing for her friends' hands and leading them through jumping and weaving around the room to the music.

By the time it ended and they paused the music again, she was thoroughly out of breath, staggering over to flop onto Lani's bed. Megan stayed there for a moment, breathing and thinking. She sat up and looked at Lani intently. "Get Cassia. I have a plan."

Chapter 34: Implementing the Plan

Most of Friday night and much of Saturday morning was spent in preparation. Lani stayed up past when the rest went to bed, working with various springs and an old alarm clock, managing to finish the project in time to get a little sleep.

Kerr showed up right on schedule on Saturday morning, with breakfast for everyone in hand. Convincing Kerr to take part took some doing and involved bringing Mr. Kahale in on the effort. He wasn't happy that the girls and Justin were putting themselves back into danger, but he also couldn't come up with anything better and agreed that both they, and Kerr, would have the menehune contingent's support.

After breakfast, they set out, following Ashling's lead. Kerr took the first step in the plan, moving to convince the other brownies to see that Megan and the rest would have assistance and messengers anywhere, even if they needed to come and go quietly. Additionally, Kerr moved to deliver a message to a few of Cassia's friends, despite some nervousness at doing so. Thus a few of the Unseelie knew they were coming, but the group wasn't met by Orlaith's guards and escorted into any sort of 'protective custody' until the Dance. So across the green lawn, in the chilled but gold-suffused air, they walked. Cassia and Justin simply wore their armor, but Lani was decked out in her mechanic's costume, and Megan was Red Riding Hood.

The walk through the halls of An Teach Deiridh were different from the last trip. From the start, the place was ridiculously crowded. Faeries of sorts she hadn't even seen yet were crowded in alongside even more of the population she did recognize. There were guards posted at the ballroom doors and those of all major rooms. Pixies and sprites flitted about over the heads of the bigger folk, delivering messages or keeping an eye on things. With all of the pixies flitting about, Megan knew they had to move fast. They were met by some of Cassia's friends, who, along with the satyress and her leopards, helped clear a path through the halls until they were in the distinctly Unseelie wing. From there, Megan headed for Riocard's room.

Once they were into the darker halls, various groups of Unseelie tried to approach them. Some looked especially threatening to Megan, though she didn't know whether they were aware of the Queen's plans and blaming Megan for her help with the sword, or just interested in the taste of princess. Thankfully, between Cassia and her friends, none of those got particularly close.

The second group seemed to be wanting to offer help with whatever she wanted to do. Rumors were circling, and in the Unseelie ranks, that made for a lot of anger at the Queen, but no real unity or organization regarding doing anything about it. Some just wanted someone to take their frustrations out on, others were clearly ready to do something, but had no plan for what that something should be. She guessed that the dungeons were full as well, until after the Dance, at least.

Cassia warned away a few of those seeming to want to offer aid, while telling others to come talk to her and where she'd be. Megan wasn't sure of the difference between who she told what, but Megan felt that Cassia could navigate this better than she would herself.

Regardless, they were able to get to their destination, her father's room. Just before she entered, she noticed a will o' wisp floating nearby. While she was pretty certain that the Queen and her guard weren't going to approach them in Riocard's room, she was far less certain of the Gray Lady. Likewise, she knew that even among the Unseelie, the Queen had her contacts and allies. Likely as not, some of them would be pretending to oppose the Queen's plans but would sabotage anything Megan tried to do.

And indeed, just as they'd gotten everyone into the room, the figure came in the doorway. Tarnished silver hair, pearl-streaked skin, empty eyes—the Gray Lady stared.

"I wanted to tell you…I am sorry your quest…backfired," the wisps whispered.

"Yeah," Megan said. "It did."

"I also simply wanted to...let you know something," the whispers continued. "Sometimes it is better to wait things out. Rash action could endanger my people."

"Our people," Megan interrupted. She may have accepted that she probably should try not to fit in all the way, all the time, but if she was going to be hearing creepy veiled threats, she wasn't going to let herself be painted as just a foreigner, too.

"Our people. I would advise against endangering them further. Waiting...one gets used to it."

"I'll keep that in mind, thanks," Megan said blankly.

The pearl-mottled face lowered in a nod, and the tarnished figure and adjacent points of light withdrew from the closing doorway.

After that, they settled into the room. There was occasional commotion at the doors, and Cassia moved to meet with some of her friends, assuring them there was a plan, and either making sure they'd know when to help Megan and company get out of An Teach Deiridh, or telling a select few that they'd be welcome to go along to help in the eventual effort. Regardless what else she told them, she wouldn't tell anyone the plans or where they were going. While Cassia tended to the door, Lani went searching through the room for anything potentially useful for the trip. "Justin," Lani said as she pointed to one of the swords on the wall. He nodded and took it, slipping it into the ornate sheath of the Claiomh Solais.

Megan and Ashling were going through papers around the piano, seeking more clues and useful songs, when nervous-looking brownies arrived with lunch and, as requested, extra food. The group packed up as soon as they felt as equipped and ready as possible.

On cue, selections of Cassia's associates caused small disturbances throughout the castle, drawing guards. Only then did Cassia and the chariot come barreling out of Riocard's room, followed closely by Justin. It wasn't long before they developed a following. Some of those who gathered up around them were those Cassia invited. Others quickly took up the cause, or just started running along out of curiosity or the odd spirit of the mob.

Regardless, by the time they reached the front doors, they had a chaotic momentum that the handful of guards left weren't going to stop. There was a bit of scuffling, but Cassia, Justin, and most of the Unseelie mob reached the doors and began the rush towards the wood where the sword was held. Pixies and other winged things rushed above them, some following the mob, some racing ahead of it to warn and reinforce the defenders.

As soon as the rushing footfalls, shouts and chariot wheels were off in the distance, Ashling peeked her head out the door. She finally gestured. "Come on, I know a back way out. Just keep it quiet." She jumped onto the Count's back, and the crow took off through the twisting hallways.

Space-mechanic Lani and Red-Riding-Megan followed, hugging the walls as best they could while keeping pace. "Are you sure the compass is going to work?" Red-Riding-Megan asked, while trying to keep the crow in sight.

"Between this and a pixie guiding us, we should be able to find him, no matter what enchantments and illusions are up around that cave, yes."

"Did you find anything in the room in case we run into guards? The Queen will be watching the cave, too."

"Not that either of us could use. We'll just have to be sneaky and hope Justin and Cassia buy us enough time."

Chapter 35: Charge for the Sword

It wasn't long before Cassia and Justin hit resistance. The Unseelie had a knack for chaotic charges, but there was a lot of ground to cover, and by appearances, the Queen had been prepared for just this. As soon as they hit covered ground, bands of soldiers appeared to engage them, or to trap one or two stragglers and fall back into the woods. Sometimes sheer numbers and enthusiasm fought them off, sometimes they thinned the pack a small amount with success, and sometimes, members of Cassia's troop gave chase, lowering her numbers more. It wasn't long before the woods rang with the sounds of battle.

Justin shouted a warning and raised his new shield, wincing only slightly. Pixie arrows mostly bounced off the metal, with a few sticking into it, hitting with more force than he'd have imagined possible for such tiny projectiles. Cassia growled off the words of a protective enchantment, not against the arrows themselves—those stuck neatly into her flesh in a few places, along with a number striking the cats. Her invigoration spell fought off the sleeping spells on the arrows, letting her and the cats keep moving through the hail of projectiles, all of the trio looking angrier than before the spell was cast.

Others in their force were less fortunate, with Unseelie falling around them. Some resisted as Cassia did, or dodged to cover, or had their own means of protection, but the numbers fell further still. By the time a host of the moth-winged sprites engaged Orlaith's pixies in a fierce aerial battle, Cassia had less than half of the people she started with.

Most of those remaining still made for a dangerous and enthusiastic band with no signs of pausing. It was all Justin could do to keep up with the crowd, doing his best to keep his shield at the ready and trusting in his armor's effectiveness against the tiny arrows as he raced along behind Cassia. He wasn't precisely sure of their directions, but thought the wood around them was starting to look familiar.

His suspicions were confirmed when sidhe knights emerged from cover at the edge of a clearing, forming up in ranks. More pixies and sprites emerged from the trees all around, aiming their bows at the oncoming mad rush. Cassia leaned forward, cutting the tethers binding the leopards to the chariot so they could maneuver and fight freely, while she just ducked down and rode out the wild ride, leaping out to engage a knight in close combat at the last second. Her chariot crashed into the assembled ranks on its own, and the leopards took up protective positions at their mistress's flanks.

The mob just behind her slammed into the ranks on the ground, while those suited to flight or climbing took to the trees to engage the archers. Justin thought he saw a weak point in the defensive lines and rushed for it, leading with the shield and battering a knight to the ground. As he did, he could see the sword and stone in the middle of the clearing, an honor guard, more decorated than most of the knights, standing around it on watch.

Before he could break free and rush them, the ranks closed, and he was forced backwards, only barely avoiding injury by spear. The faeries around him were nearly invulnerable, at least in the sense that they'd heal almost anything that wasn't made by cold iron—which no one here seemed to be using—but Justin had no such assurance.

He retreated backwards as his assailants were engaged by some sort of troll swinging a small tree like a club. He had to dive out of the way of the swinging tree himself, reminded that his allies had, possibly, even less regard for him in some cases than his enemies of the moment. He made his way back to Cassia and the leopards. The cats let him into their defensive circle, and the satyr, despite her wild, powerful fighting style and obvious rage, shifted to allow him to fight alongside her.

Even with all of his training, he had to admit that it was fortunate. Most of the sidhe clearly had many decades, if not centuries, of training behind them. Fighting almost purely defensively, and with the savage satyr and the leopards forcing opponents to be cautious, he was able to manage to protect himself, but unable to advance.

Cassia seemed to be having better luck. Even hit with several more pixie arrows and engaged by multiple sidhe knights, she managed to slowly force her opponents back. Justin shifted after her, making slow progress, but progress towards the goal nonetheless. While some of the Unseelie horde were being pushed back, others, such as the troll who had provided him cover, were making similar steps forward, pushing the sidhe back bit by bit.

It was only once they'd broken past the treeline, forcing the knights fully into the clearing, that the situation became much worse. More sidhe emerged from the trees. Some of them were further knights, but these, instead of joining the ranks, protected individuals who were in lighter garb, and chanting. Justin stepped back on seeing them, taking cover behind a tree.

A blast of fire slammed into the chest of the troll, sending it flying back with a shockwave that followed. Bursts of light flashed all over the battlefield, emitting from behind the lines of the knights so only the attackers would be blinded. Justin hid his eyes only just in time. Numerous of the Unseelie weren't as fortunate. More fireballs launched into the Unseelie ranks, taking their own toll. Even when they missed their mark, the shockwaves that followed scattered the ranks of the Unseelie, forcing more of them to either retreat back into the woods or remain close to the ranks of the knights, which presented its own dangers.

Some of the Unseelie attempted to counter with their own enchantments. Greenish fireballs fired back, briar vines started to grow at the edge of the wood, and wisps of darkness started to creep onto the field, all heading for the knights. As soon as any of the enchantments reached the field, they weakened or disappeared entirely. The fireballs fizzled, or dwindled to small missiles which only left small scorch marks on armor. The briars wilted to something sidhe swords easily sliced through, and the darkness dissipated at the next flash of light. With the time they'd had to prepare, the Queen had clearly added plenty of protective enchantments to the clearing. She might not be able to do much to the sword itself, but the ground between the woods and the blade was another matter entirely. He realized, at the same time, that if they'd had time to put up the defenses, who knew what else they'd prepared.

"Cassia, we need to fall back!" he shouted over the din of battle.

Whirling, slashing, and kicking, Cassia, Maxwell at her side, showed no signs of being willing to give up an inch of the ground she'd gained. Jude took notice, moving to help protect Justin as the squire lunged back into the melee, despite the risks, knocking aside one of the sidhe spearmen trying to find an opening to stab at Cassia. "We need to retreat!" he shouted again.

Cassia growled at him instead, and with fewer Unseelie venturing beyond the edges of the woods, he noticed that the sidhe ranks were closing in around them, and more carefully aimed arrows were coming their way, only barely fended off by armor and Cassia's own enchantments. He turned to cover her back, fighting back to back with her, with the leopards guarding the pair, all whirling and moving and slashing at anything that came too close, while their opponents tried to trap them.

Justin took a spear to the side. His armor kept it from being worse than a scratch, but he could still feel the warm trickle of blood down his skin. His counter-slash broke the spear before it could do more harm. He managed to fend off the first efforts to close in and take advantage of the wound. Between the pain and the fatigue of the long run and the battle, he almost missed the next detail. When the knights gave up on trying to take him down, they retreated, but further back than they had been. A quick glance confirmed that the rest of the knights around them were falling back too, with a few spears trying to prevent Cassia from following them.

Dropping his sword, he grabbed for the back of Cassia's armor and pulled. Not expecting the grab, he caught her off balance, and was dragging her backwards towards the wood when the fireball hit where they'd just been standing. He registered heat washing over him, but without any hint of pain. The shockwave was something else entirely. He held on tight to Cassia as he, she, and both cats were launched back into the woods.

Landing heavily, he tried to pull her back further under cover, with a few more of the Unseelie closing around them defensively. Cassia sat up groggily after a few moments. "We need to retreat, now," Justin repeated. "We did everything we could. We have to rely on the others now."

"And keep these lot busy with a chase," Cassia agreed, shaking off the cobwebs. The whistle that followed was met with an answering growl and whine. Noticing the cause for distress, Justin found the spot Jude had dragged Maxwell to, both burned and bleeding, but the bareheaded cat far worse off and not moving. He confirmed that Max was still breathing, then lifted the leopard over his shoulders. Jude limped after him as Cassia rallied her troops, regrouping those who would listen to form up for a fighting retreat, leaving the sword behind.

Chapter 36: Quest for the King

Ashling led the girls in costume on a circuitous route. Even with her help, they ended up having to hide several times in order to avoid various patrols. Seelie or Unseelie, it didn't matter. Cassia and Justin were out for attention, while the smaller group needed to evade both the Queen's people and the Gray Lady's. Much as the Gray Lady had come and gone quickly with just a word of warning, they'd been sure that it had, indeed, been a warning, and sending the raiding party after the sword definitely hadn't been quiet, or patient.

The need for stealth slowed them down; the extension to their route slowed progress further. At the very least, both were relieved when they reached the foothills, even if the walk became more difficult. In matters regarding Riocard, they'd been pretty sure the pixie would stay focused and take them the right direction—but with Ashling, it was never a sure thing until a task was complete.

The walk turned into a climb, occasionally treacherous, moving up nearly vertical stretches of rocks and hoping for the stability of handholds, whether in the rocks, or of the various climbing vines or small trees growing amidst the rocks. Lani had recovered their gear from the previous trip and restocked. This left them with heavier packs, but at least they had rope and climbing tools, making the way a little easier for whoever was taking their turn trailing the other, once they managed each stretch.

A couple of times, on seeing caves or dark recesses in the rock, they thought they were nearing the end of their journey, but each time, the crow passed it by and kept climbing, occasionally circling back to make sure the girls hadn't been lost.

The biggest problem, eventually, turned out to not be the difficulty of the climb, or the exhaustion of doing so, but the exposed nature of the mountain faces. Without cover, and having to move slowly, it turned out to be inevitable they'd eventually be seen. They were nearly knocked from the cliff face they were climbing when a burst of fire impacted the stone behind them, a shockwave following the explosion. Lani just managed to roll up over the top of the current expanse onto level ground, and grabbed for her friend's wrist before the impact shook her free.

Though they had covered a lot of ground, it now didn't seem nearly high, or far enough, and they picked up on signs of flying dots in the distance coming their way, leaving them pretty certain that pixie arrows were going to be a problem soon. Adrenaline took over, and the pair launched themselves back up the mountainside, moving with less caution than before in their haste to get to cover without being trapped. The haste almost caused a couple of falls, as untested handholds gave way, but each time, quick rescues were made, or the second grab found something more solid.

"This way!" Ashling finally called, the first thing she'd said in ages, as Red-Riding-Megan was pulling herself up over another cliff face and onto a longer stretch of mostly level ground, dotted with sharp rock outcroppings. When she reached down to help Lani, a small dart missed her hand by inches, embedding into the rock. Another two found homes in nearby plants. "Hurry!" she called down.

Lani was hurrying her best, but was having trouble reaching a couple of the handholds. Nearly being hit with a couple of pixie arrows from the oncoming archers wasn't helping. "Go on!" she shouted. "Get to cover." This was ignored, and soon rope got Lani up the last bit.

They were almost to the rocks when Lani screamed, tumbling over, clutching at her calf, where one of the arrows was embedded. With help, she dragged herself behind the rocks, struggling to stay awake. As soon as they had brief protection from the rocks, she went through her pack with increasingly numb hands. She needed help to get the caffeine boost gum out of the pack, unable to manage the finesse of the wrappers. She didn't at all care for the faux-energy-drink artificial taste, but the gum helped, if only barely.

A glance back over the rocks confirmed the pixies closing in. Gambling, Red-Riding-Megan wrapped the cloak around her and stood, doing her best to belt out the lyrics to a song. Out of breath and frantic, nothing magical happened, but at this height, the pixies, who may have heard of the experience with the winds in the clearing, or even been there, were taking no chances. The butterfly winged patrols scattered, ducking and diving for something to hold on to.

In the brief lull, both girls took off as fast as they could manage after Ashling. "You're sure that thing is going to work?"

"If we can make it to the cave," Lani called back, having a rough time managing to dig the compass out of her pocket as they scrambled.

"It's right up there!" Ashling shouted back to them, darting around a bend.

A handful of tiny arrows hit the rocks behind them, another punching a hole through one side of the red cape, entangling in the fabric without hitting flesh. Even with the renewed rush of panicked energy at being shot at, Lani barely managed to stay upright, lurching and almost falling before catching herself on an outcropping. "Keep going," she tried again.

The other two turned back for her anyway, though she needed some additional support to walk in a straight line, struggling to stay awake as they walked, focusing on Ashling's assurances that the cave was close now.

Two moth-winged shapes streaked by overhead, racing for the cave without any attempt at firing at the girls, just to warn whoever was on guard inside. As they moved, there was another out-of-breath attempt at singing. This time, with level ground to fall onto if things went badly, or having noted the earlier failure, the patrols behind them barely slowed down.

The cave entrance came into view, a huge, icy maw in the midst of gray stone. They could see the jagged, reflective surfaces just inside, and numerous possible passages into the cave. Lani clutched tightly at her compass, gesturing with the other arm which way they should be headed as they made the cave mouth, while being almost pulled along by her friend as much as she was managing to run on her own.

Lani went dead weight as another arrow jabbed into her shoulder, and the compass hit the ground, rolling and clattering along on the stone. Ashling doubled back, landing and shouting encouragement, but couldn't offer much more help while Lani was dragged along. They just made the mouth of the cave ahead of more arrows, taking cover, and starting to head in the direction Lani had been pointing, when figures emerged from the darkness within the cave. Pixies and sprites landed, or hovered behind them as they stopped, several armed figures emerging from various passages to block their way.

The mixture of lightly armored knights and redcaps made for a motley alliance, but at least for the moment, they were working in obvious unison. Peadar took the lead of the group, spinning his bat around in one hand, his grin just getting bigger and bigger as he approached the girl in the red cloak.

"Well, well, well, what do we have here? I'm impressed you made it this far. Good job. Afraid you're not going to be rescuing Riocard today, though. Unless..." he paused, as a thought occurred to him. "Unless you want to call that favor in?"

Around the cave, hands on weapons tensed as the sidhe, redcaps, pixies, and sprites all glanced at each other nervously, suddenly uncertain of the alliance, and who would turn what way if Peadar mutinied for the sake of seeing his debt canceled.

Ashling took the moment to drag the compass back over, lifting it with a strain, and shoving it upwards, determined to see Riocard rescued. Pulling her cloak around her a little tighter, Red-Riding-Megan made an effort to wake Lani up, in hopes of getting her advice, while the silence and uncertainty in the cave stretched on. With Lani still fast asleep, she finally looked down at Ashling and her compass, then up at the lead redcap, and shook her head. "No, no. Not now. We surrender."

Chapter 37: The Dance

Despite the apparent dimensions of the grand ballroom and the sheer numbers of faeries gathered, even with the distractions, the room kept taking more guests, with enough room for everyone to dance or watch from the walls. Elevated recesses lined the walls, providing smaller dancing or spectating space for the pixies, sprites, and others, so the smaller folk could stay out from underfoot.

Faeries of both courts were gathered, but even amidst the tension earlier in the day, the enchantments on the room prevented violence. Some members of both courts mingled, while others kept to their own. Muttering grew as the first skirmishers from the chaotic fight earlier arrived. A group of sidhe knights led a number of prisoners into the room, marching up to the Queen where she sat on the grand chair at the head of the room. "The scouts report the fight is still going, but we captured these. What should be done with them?" the highest ranking knight asked.

Orlaith waved a hand dismissively. "Release them. This is an exciting time of year. They're surely just getting some energy out. I trust no one has been seriously injured?"

"A few lost limbs, eyes, and wings are the worst of it. Everyone will recover. No sign of cold iron," he reported, guessing at the Queen's meaning.

Orlaith nodded. "Very well then, just a bit of fun. Set up an extra patrol of the doors, and make sure those brought in from the scuffle don't head back out to it."

Both the knights and the prisoners being released bowed to the Queen. There were a few glares exchanged between both ranks, but that was the extent of it, before the knights moved to reinforce the watch at the main doors, while the Unseelie who'd followed in Cassia's wake filtered out onto the ballroom floor.

More of the groups were brought in, some unconscious, delivered to some part of their delegation, some on their own, simply filtering back after their excitement died down, some in chains—released as soon as they reached the ballroom. After the first few, it became routine, with many groups barely taking notice.

That changed, commotion rising again, when a small band made their way in. While they were accompanied by a number of sidhe knights from the door guard, Cassia, Justin and the small band with them had all arrived free. Jude and the now-conscious Maxwell limped along at Cassia's sides, helping lead the small procession. Cassia marched towards the Queen. Despite the enchantments on the room, her glare was sufficient that of the accompanying knights and the Queen's guard, only General Inwar didn't put a hand to a sword hilt. Orlaith remained relaxed, lifting a brow and waiting.

Just as Cassia was about to speak, a greater commotion arose from the halls outside. All heads, including Cassia's, turned to try to figure out what the new disturbance was. Peadar led a band of mixed sidhe and redcaps, walking to escort Megan on either side. A crow was on one shoulder, a pixie on the other, and a groggy-looking Lani alongside. The red hood was pulled over her head, and she walked, head bowed in defeat. They were led up to the grand chair. Cassia's scowl grew deeper still, seeing the prisoners.

The Queen waved off the escort, smiling pleasantly as the girls were led to the front of the room. "So good to have you with us, Princess. And just in time. The Dance is about to begin. It would have been a shame had you missed it."

The red hood dipped lower, with no answer. Cassia tensed, but made no move. Justin stepped in, placing a hand on the red-caped shoulder, while Jude padded up next to Lani, nudging at her. Lani sighed, petting the leopard.

"Your father is supposed to be here any time now." This time, Cassia was clearly running into the enchantments on the room, straining a few moments, before settling for just glaring daggers at the Queen. Orlaith continued, not reacting or even looking at the satyr. "It's not like him to miss a party."

As she spoke, the Queen stood, walking down the steps and towards the open ballroom floor. The girls stepped aside, but Cassia and Maxwell held their ground. It was hard to tell which was growling more. Inwar finally moved, stepping down after the Queen, and a few of the guards closed in. Orlaith just waited, smiling pleasantly, while Cassia snarled and glared. "Surely you're not going to interfere with the Dance," Orlaith finally said.

Cassia looked about to say something, then finally stepped aside, dragging Maxwell along with her, allowing the Queen to pass. Orlaith stepped out onto the empty ballroom floor as the music began, waiting for her absent partner. Whispers and murmurs arose around the room, with numerous faeries looking around, and more than a few peeking out into the hallways.

Orlaith waited patiently, eyes on the doorway, unmoving. Finally, when the murmurs started to build in intensity, she spoke, cutting off the building commentary. "My fellows—" all eyes turned to her, and the room went quiet, aside from the music. As she was about to continue her concerned announcement, footsteps echoed through the halls outside. The sidhe knights stationed outside the ballroom moved inside, and into ceremonial position.

The figure who entered the room was in full armor for the occasion, six and a half feet tall of woven branches, covered in wicked thorns. A bejeweled ceremonial sword rested at one hip. The crowd parted, leaving a wide path open for the King to approach the dance floor and his partner.

Orlaith stepped forward. Neither her surprise nor her plans were relevant. Her partner was here. There were rules.

As was proper, a slow song began in 2/2 time, on a snare drum accompanied by a lute. As was proper, they formally progressed towards each other in 'hesitation steps,' like members of bridal parties walking down the aisle. They met at the center of the room, and each dancer raised an open palm.

As was particularly proper for the Seelie and Unseelie courts on their day of transition, the delicate glove and the briar gauntlet never quite met. The onlooking courts were used to seeing it, of course. It had certainly nothing to do with concern over physical delicacy or roughness. The always-half-an-inch of space between Orlaith's and Riocard's hands might as well have been a magnetic repulsion field—or maybe a field that was simply kept in flux, its attraction thwarted. Those who knew the King and Queen wouldn't necessarily be surprised.

Central to such a dance, of course, is the eye contact. The courts were used to this as well. But those watching the Queen this night saw something unusual as she stared past the mask, a series of flashes in her eyes: surprise, anger, appreciation, acceptance, and a return to the smooth decorum of the occasion.

As was ever proper, they made their way through formal steps in a slow procession. Each set of steps wove them in little curves of circles around each other, but all gradually took them towards the throne.

The steps were perfectly timed so that the briarmailed figure, in circling around Orlaith, reached the throne, offered her a low bow which Orlaith returned in a curtsey, and in the final notes of the song, sat.

As both courts stared in silence, full of unasked questions aside from certain exceptions, the briarmail began to slowly unravel from itself. Something in the air glistened as it did, as if the size and shape of the heavily enchanted armor had become...warped. And as the briarmail boots and legs spun their way apart, they revealed tennis shoes. Tennis shoes that belonged to someone far shorter than 6 feet. The gauntlets next fell away to reveal smaller, dexterous, lightly freckled hands. The mask and the rest of the briars unwound in turn, revealing a Seahawks cap, red hair, green eyes, and, in general, Megan O'Reilly.

Chapter 38: Return of the King

Even indoors, the effect on the season was obvious. A cold wind whipped through the open windows, chilling the ballroom. The near-tangible light that had suffused everything faded, replaced by a more natural moonlight, and after a few moments, a light fog rolled all the way into the ballroom. Megan felt a moment of invigoration and could feel a pull from the throne under her — the ballroom had accepted her.

Between her previous preparatory dancing lessons, Megan had learned that once the claim was established, she didn't have to stay in position the whole time. So she rose from the great chair and from the remainder of the suit, which had felt vaguely like trying to dance on stilts, but otherwise comfortable.

Confusion rippled through the room, with any number of reactions evident, but no one moved. Orlaith herself seemed to be taking the defeat far more gracefully than Megan had feared. Indeed, the Queen looked as if she'd gained a measure of respect for Megan, judging by her light smile and the look in her eyes. Orlaith curtseyed to the current...Unseelie Queen pro tempore? Autumn Regent? Megan had the chair; she did not have a grasp of the terminology. At any rate, the definitely-a-Queen, who was no longer currently reigning, went to stand with her General, who was looking about.

Megan looked around, too, noting some of the other changes in the room. The first and most obvious was Cassia. The satyress was grinning with every bit as much intensity as she'd glared before — the same intensity that had done a masterful job keeping the Queen from paying too much attention to others before her.

The next glance, as Megan stepped over, was for Red-Riding-Megan. For a moment, the twins stared at each other, before the Megan in the red cloak started to shift, the illusion falling away as she became much less obviously a she, and the androgynous form of Kerr took Red-Riding-Megan's place.

The brownie awkwardly removed a makeshift amulet made from elements of a first-aid kit and offered it to Megan. "Here'syourbloodback, Highness," Kerr muttered.

With a lot of eyes on the brownie, Kerr shuffled nervously from foot to foot. Kerr seemed about to say something else to Megan, mouth opening and closing. Then there was a glance to the Queen, looking apologetic and nervous, but still finding no words. Finally, Kerr looked at Lani, and flashed the little 'secret handshake' the two had shared before. Waking up a little, Lani returned the sign. Treaty and friendship acknowledged, but clearly still uncertain of anything beyond wanting desperately to be out of the spotlight, Kerr darted towards Maxwell to start tending to the leopard's wounds.

Lani got a hug from Megan. Not entirely dignified, but in Megan's mind, both necessary, and somehow appropriate that the Unseelie Princess…whatever of the moment be allowed her lapses in dignity even at the most obviously ceremonial moments.

She looked around for Ashling and the Count, to find the crow, with the pixie on his back, had perched on one arm of the great chair. Ashling made a gesture to the seat, obviously suggesting Megan should get back to business. Megan paused long enough to give each of the leopards a quick scratch, then went back up the steps. Just as she was about to sit, an even colder wind went through the room, and the howling of the wind briefly sounded almost like fanfare. As the wind faded, a chocolatey smooth voice called from the doorway, "I do believe that's my chair."

Megan blushed, looking around at all of the courts gathered around the room. She could still feel the great chair and its pull, but it was almost a relief to step aside, curtseying as formally as she could manage, and gesturing to the great chair, though she remained on the dais.

Riocard's coal-black hair ran wild down his back, and ice-blue eyes shown inhumanly iridescent from his oddly-angled face as he walked across the ballroom, winds carrying his whispers to Megan alone. "I'm certain your first royal decree was going to be to see me freed. With the surge in power from the changing of the season, I thought I'd handle that myself and save you the trouble. But thank you. Judging by Orlaith's face, I'd have to guess it was artfully done. You'll have to sing me the story."

Megan's grin grew as he spoke to her, becoming wider still as her father came up the steps of the dais and touched his armor. The vines wound around him, overlaying his ragged hunting clothes, covering him from head to toe until he touched the forehead with two fingertips, and the helmet portion unwound. The proper Unseelie King took his seat and looked out at his court.

"I'm sorry I'm late," were his first words to the assembled. "But it sounds like my daughter has been keeping you all entertained. And, speaking of my daughter, my season's boon on taking power is due. So for this year, my favor from the realm is... regardless of your feelings towards today's drama, all guilt for today's actions are upon me, and I hereby pardon myself without exception. No action is to be taken against her or her friends, mortal or faerie. They are under my absolute protection, and the realm will help to enforce the decree that any who seek revenge or harm against them do so against my wishes, and they will be banished to a certain cave of ice, to reside within a circle of salt for a century and a day. I trust I'm clear."

It was abundantly clear to Megan. After all the risks she'd taken, the gesture was obviously not only one of her father's regard for her, but his way of paying any debt he owed before anyone sought to make him say he owed her one. At once, she both realized she had no intention of doing so, and that he'd have entirely respected it had that been her first commentary to him. She was surprised, at first, how quickly that seemed to settle the matter in the court. Even some of those who looked the most irate at her little surprise looked much more relaxed now.

Riocard continued, having made his pronouncement, "Now then, critical business attended to, I have a question for all of you." He grinned, shifting from a formal position on the throne to leaning back against one arm at an angle, so he could put his legs up across the other arm of the chair, and gesture casually towards the room, looking far more at home now, "Why isn't anyone dancing? It's a party, after all."

At his words, the music began, and faeries of all sorts and sizes and descriptions took to the floor, closing ranks to find partners, starting to dance and whirl and jump amidst the low fog that had filled the room.

Orlaith still stood calmly with her general. Riocard looked to her, strangely intent but not hostile at all. "You'll save me the gavotte later, Majesty?" he called to her.

"Always, Majesty," the Seelie Queen called back.

Finally, everything seemed right and comfortable in the realm... until Megan realized the song choice, doing a double take as she ensured she heard it right. After the formal dance of the change of power, the first dance of Riocard's seasonal reign was 'Yet Another Song About Jumping.'

Chapter 39: Resolutions and Revelations

After the party, Riocard was taking audiences. Megan stood at this side and watched, while Ashling and the Count remained perched on the arm of the chair, looking quite comfortable with the arrangement, aside from what Megan was pretty certain was a brief narrowing of eyes at the Gray Lady's back. The Unseelie may not so much forgive and forget, as just remember and forgive anyway, outside of keeping a closer eye on the suspected, but Ashling was still Seelie, after all.

"Counts-to-18," Riocard said suddenly. "What's putting a rough edge on our Ashling's good mood?"

"Caw."

"Well, I don't see how it isn't your place to say," the Unseelie King debated casually. "You were asked the question."

Megan, intending to save the crow and the pixie embarrassment—and have any reason to talk to her dad more—decided to explain. "We think the Gray Lady helped Orlaith coordinate the ambush and everything."

"...Oh?" Riocard asked as the room got quieter.

Megan nodded. "She didn't want you rescued. Seems like she thinks you're too irresponsible and that the way to keep everyone out of danger was to let the Queen win."

The tarnished figure turned. The empty eyes stared.

"Riocard, I didn't—" the haunted whispers began.

"Of course you didn't, old friend," the chocolatey voice said calmly. His smile was easy, too easy.

The Gray Lady stood blankly for a moment, then left in silence, her lights flickering around her.

Riocard remained silent for a moment, staring at the door.

"Are you going looking for her?" Megan asked. "To stop her or...or arrest her...?" Though nobody seemed to stay arrested around here.

"Of course not. I can't go running out of my own audience. And revenge is just inefficient for people like us. Besides, she's always been in pain. I ... can guess a little, at how it must feel," he said slowly, with a look at Megan that was the closest she'd seen on him to worried. "But of course, I have hopes to never know for sure what real grief, real loss, feels like." He smiled. "It just wouldn't be my style."

Megan was still reflecting on all this when her father spoke again. "Justin of Ludlow."

"Your Majesty," Justin replied, stepping forward, and dropping to one knee, head bowed.

"I've come to understand that you put yourself at great risk helping to carry out my daughter's plan. Now, just to be certain, you do understand you'd already paid off all obligation to Faerie and its royalty, yes?"

"I do, Your Majesty."

"Then why return? You've no kin here."

"I need no kin involved to protect the world," he paused, "Or Megan or Lani. They've helped me."

"And it's what a brave knight would do, yes?"

"I'm no knight, not even quite old enough, but I'd like to think so."

"Age is just a number—albeit a very large number in some of our cases. I've known plenty of humans who called themselves knights. Most of them had neither your conviction nor courage. That's good enough for me." He drew the jeweled sword, pondering it, and finally stood. "Now, let's see, I've seen Orlaith do this plenty of times." He glanced at Ashling. "How did that first part go?"

"By the Power of Grayskull," she offered helpfully.

"Ah, yes," Riocard answered with a smile, returning his attention to Justin. "By right of being king, and the power entrusted to me by the court, I declare your trials at an end. You are a knight of two realms, and one of the few mortals welcome in Faerie. You are now Sir Justin of Ludlow." He tapped the sword on each of Justin's shoulders. "Or Seattle, if you like. I do recommend the place. Now, rise. You have a lot of...knightly...things...to do, yes. Start with fetching the Claiomh Solais. It has better things to do, and it would be rather inconvenient for those without the sheath to try to get it, even if I had another proper human on hand, which I don't. Besides, you've proven yourself capable. I think you should keep it."

Justin's eyes went wide, glancing at the sheath. Then he bowed. "Of course, Majesty," he responded, before rising to his feet.

"Good," Riocard said as he sat again, gesturing with casual dismissal. "You'll fit in fine, clearly having plenty of court experience. We're just like any other court, only more so."

Justin nodded as he backed away, and started looking around at the court.

Riocard moved on, gesturing to Cassia. Cassia stepped up, flanked by the leopards. Maxwell looked somewhat more of a twin for his brother than usual, decked out in head bandaging, expertly applied by Kerr. The satyr bowed before Riocard.

"I've been hearing rumors you caused quite the stir yesterday," he offered her, with a grin. "The healers have been working through the night." A pause, before he added, "Well done."

"Thank you. I live to serve."

"No doubt, then, you'll be glad to hear you get to keep on serving. I trust you won't mind giving the Princess a hand now and then, seeing as you're neighbors?"

Cassia glanced at Megan and grinned. "No problem at all."

"Good, then go have a chat with the Huntsman and have him get the Wild Hunt ready. I've heard you and the hounds got acquainted already, so you won't mind leading the hunt, as soon as your companions are suitably healed. Tell him that I said you get to pick the subject of the hunt."

Megan suddenly felt very sorry for someone or something, but wasn't about to ask. Cassia grinned savagely, gesturing for the leopards to follow as she turned and walked out of the room.

Lani followed, taking her turn as Riocard paid his debts without once mentioning obligations or favors. "Ahhh, not always one of my greatest fans," Riocard said with a smile. "Thank you."

"It was necessary," Lani replied, still looking tired, but pleased with the results of the day.

"Your family has always been very good with necessary. I can appreciate that. It sometimes sounds too tedious for me to quite comprehend, but it's good that someone is. And...yes, family. You're very close."

"We are," Lani agreed, looking a little more cautious.

"Commendable," Riocard said. "Then your father has the winter off, to see to whatever projects he likes. I think we can manage here. And your little brother...will fall under my earlier decree of protection as well. I trust that suits?"

Lani's caution turned to relief. Her shoulders slumped, and Megan could see her struggling to maintain her composure and not start tearing up. Megan wasn't quite sure why Lani'd gotten so quickly worried about Mack, but she rescued her friend, stepping up to give Lani a hug until Lani had a few seconds to compose herself. "Yes, yes. Thank you, Majesty," she responded.

"Oh, and then there's Kerr," Riocard began. "First and foremost, I think your friend has had quite enough stress and attention for the day. The next time you see Kerr, though, please pass on that I think a promotion is in order, should Kerr want to pick a kitchen to be in charge of." Lani nodded and stepped back.

Megan ascended the dais again, and was the only one close enough to hear Riocard addressing Ashling and the Count. "And the two of you? What would you like?"

Megan was startled, finally hearing him at least acknowledge a sense of indebtedness to anyone, but got the feeling that the intense loyalty of the pixie was returned.

"Caw, caw."

"Yes, Count, that can be arranged. I shall procure a bust of Pallas for my chambers forthwith." His gaze turned to the pixie.

"Make that two," she said. "One for your room, and one for Megan's. Because I'm going back with Megan."

"You're certain? There is still the matter of the Ellén Trechend hunt left unfinished."

Ashling hesitated, then grinned. "Okay, so right after that, I'm going back. She can probably manage without me for a few days. But she has so much to learn. And I'm really good at explaining things."

"Of course you are, my friend. Of course you can go back. She'll need you."

Justin had still not left to fetch the sword. He was fidgeting slightly, staring at the far side of the room. A handful of sidhe women gathered not far from the door, talking amongst themselves.

Despite the lack of dress code, they were dressed in party finery in tones suitable for the season. Beyond the dresses, it was hard to truly differentiate them, for they all had the slightly alien beauty of the sidhe, a bit too perfect, with pale skin, eyes of impossibly bright blue or green, and hair the color of spun platinum. When they noticed Justin's looking, they smiled back in bright, manic unison.

Megan stepped off the dais to approach him. "What's wrong? You like the knight thing, right?"

"Yes. Very much. I'm proud to serve," he said. "But I know a little too much about courts, and a good bit about the fair folk on top of it. The combination...I need a favor."

"Okay, but favors get complicated, and Dad seems to be—"

"Not that kind of favor. I'm added to the court novelties. It would be... less awkward, easier to avoid offending some courtiers, if the Princess beat them to it." He lowered himself to kneel again, this time to Megan. "May I have a token from you?"

Megan blushed. "A...token from me?"

"I know you. I trust you."

"I...thanks. I trust you too." Megan sort of understood, finally. In the movies, ladies gave 'their' knights scarves, embroidered things, or occasionally flowers. "But I don't have a handkerchief or anything." She bit her lip for a moment, then grinned, stepping forward. "Sir Knight, I'm honored," she replied as she removed her Seahawks hat, placing it on Justin's head. He looked a little confused, but most of those watching just grinned, the platinum blonde sidhe ladies less so. "I hope that will do."

"Very nicely, my lady, thank you."

"And now that we're through all the knighting... just Megan, please."

"All right, my... Megan." he responded, rising again, eyes up towards the brim of the cap, still getting used to it.

"Great. Now go get your sword, so we can all go home tomorrow."

Chapter 40: Private Performance

Megan was home on time on Sunday, just before dusk set in. She assured her mother that she'd had a great Halloween with Lani, and that she'd taken her medicine already. This was true; she'd had the lower dose, some much earlier, though her mother would also see fewer of the 'orange pills' if she looked. Vitamin C was healthy.

"Hey mom," she said, as her mother was leaving her room.

"Yes, honey?"

"I was kind of thinking about taking some music lessons."

"You are. Ms. Dahl. You still have an A, right?"

"Yes. I do, but Music Appreciation and Theory isn't exactly the same as, say, voice lessons."

Her mother paused, looking at Megan for several long seconds before answering. "What brought this on? You already have your artwork."

"Well, I did a little bit of singing, just silly stuff over the holiday. I got a lot of compliments on my voice." She saw no signs of her mother's expression changing and quickly shifted tactics, "And it brought to mind that some of my teachers and the school counselor said I could use some things to kind of broaden my college applications. Never too early to start thinking about those, now that my grades are getting better. I figured, maybe, if I had a knack for it, I could take a few lessons, see about maybe joining the school choir."

Her mother's expression softened. "So this would just be school things?"

"And just trying a few private lessons, yes," she assured her mother, guessing at the reasons for worry.

"Well, all right. We can look into it. I'll ask some friends who have done some vocal training. But this would be conditional—you need to keep up with your schoolwork."

"I have my reading for English class mostly done. I'll be ready for the test on Friday," Megan assured her mother. "I'm actually kind of enjoying it. Lani has really been helping with math class too. She's really, really good at it."

"I'm glad to hear it, honey."

"Thanks. And Mom?"

"Yes?"

"Can we put up Christmas lights this year?"

"Megan, it's November 1st. But maybe once it's actually December."

"Oh, yeah, definitely not until December. Everything for the right season. Just thought I'd ask, thanks."

"Good. You're welcome. I should let you get back to studying, then. Dinner will be ready in a little more than an hour."

"I'll be ready for a break by then, thank you. And Mom?"

"Yes?"

"I love you."

"I love you too, Megan." She left, closing the door behind her.

Megan pulled the Late for the Party CD out of her bag, looking over the playlist a few moments, before tucking it back in her bag, to make sure she didn't absently start playing it at home like she was certain she would if it was kept in reach. After that, she found another CD from her collection and put some music on, quietly enough that it wouldn't bring her mother back into the room.

She cracked open the book, trying to moderate her impulses by rewarding herself for every ten minutes of reading with a bit of doodling in the margins, decorating the pages of *Romeo and Juliet* with dancing butterflies and moths and, eventually, a Queen butterfly with tattered wings, watching the dance from her crow-shaped royal throne.

Forty minutes later, with the page fully illuminated and multiple Verona residents dead, Megan needed some air. She stood, turned off the stereo, opened the window, and looked out into the twilight sky. Smelling the crisp Autumn air, she imagined she could feel the pull of Faerie. She closed her eyes, imagining different stars, imagining the low fog rolling in. She began to hum, keeping her voice low and soft.

Without opening her eyes, she trusted her memory of her room, moving through the steps of a complex dance again. The breeze picked up, and she would have sworn its whispers were singing along to the tune. When she opened her eyes, a dozen leaves had blown in through the window, laying flat on her bedroom floor.

She began to hum again, and the winds picked back up, carrying the leaves around in gentle eddies, circling and spinning as she recalled the notes. She stepped around in their midst, humming a little louder. The leaves whirled and danced around her feet, never quite touching her.

A thought hit her, and she stopped humming. The wind died down, and the leaves settled back onto the floor. She started with a quiet voice, teasing about silly, fluffy pop songs and starting to bounce and shift. Sure enough, the leaves picked up again, this time, on their own, darting and weaving around.

She paused, and again the leaves dropped. She crouched and started tying stems together, binding each set of two leaves into little wings. The song picked up again, Megan unable to resist bouncing along as she sang 'Yet Another Song About Jumping' to herself. And from even the cautious, hushed tones, the leaves picked up, and her Autumn Butterflies danced for their Princess.

Preview of *Street Fair*

Book Two in the

Fair Folk Chronicles

Chapter 1: Evaluation

"Conflict in Gaelic Cultures is a 400-level course, Mr. Thomas. They knew it was going to be difficult when they signed up." Dr. Brian O'Neill paused just long enough to let the other voice on the phone utter two and a half sentences before interrupting. "Do any of them discuss all nine salient points covered in class?" This time the pause was only for two and a half syllables before he interrupted his TA again. "Then no one earned an A. I don't think the instructions could be any clearer."

He allowed a few more words as he walked briskly through the mostly empty halls, then continued, speaking just as briskly. "All the more so for the first test of the Summer quarter. A bit of tactical advice, Mr. Thomas: always set the bar clearly high from the beginning of the term, when they still have time to do better quality work." He began the first of three flights of stairs, his free hand clutching the duffle bag over his shoulder to keep it from jostling irritatingly. "And their electing to take the class in what could have been a vacation term is commendable, but it does not change the grading standards of the university."

He was intent on not letting his breathing get too much heavier as he spoke. "I'm sure you'll handle those questions ably in your own office hours. Mine will not resume until the autumn. My current research is very time-consuming. I'll see you Monday." He hung up as he reached the third flight of stairs, then the final hallway.

Dr. O'Neill reached his office. He took a deep breath, whispered a few syllables in an old dialect of Gaelic, and shifted his foot in one shoe a little to make sure the penny he'd placed in the heel was still there, even if he'd been vaguely aware of it throughout the long walk. Caution was critical. Finally, he reached for the doorknob, turned—then paused, looking about to make sure he was actually alone, before he slipped into his office.

As he closed the door, he checked to make sure the horseshoe was still nailed perfectly above it. Over the window, he'd gone with daisy chains to complement the salt on the windowsill. He set the filthy duffel bag on the desk and opened it, removing stack after stack of damp $20 bills. His thumb brushed off some of the grime from the top bill of each stack.

He lifted one closer in the florescent light. "L-7-2..." His voice rang clear, even when just reading a serial number. "525..." Precision was important—so, so important—but it wasn't everything. "383..." He should be able to command attention if he were reading the phone book. "...B. Exactly so. For the first."

Then he replaced the bills in the bag, set it down, and took his seat at his desk.

Fifteen centuries of genealogy charts, on various qualities of paper and various things that technically were not paper at all, covered the left wall of the office. He glanced over at them, studying name after name. He looked at one of the lowest ones, printed out in a calligraphic font on multipurpose laser paper: *Brian Angus Ui Niall.*

He refocused. He opened drawers, taking out antique coins from one and an old book from another. He laid the coins out on his desk and stared a while, then carefully perused a few pages of the book. Frowning, he put the coins away. He rose and stepped over to the right wall of his office. Taking down a framed certificate, he studied it for a few moments as he returned to his seat.

This is to certify that BRIAN ANGUS O'NEILL, having submitted a thesis entitled The Wielding of Sacred Power in Ancient Ireland *and having satisfied all the conditions prescribed by the Statues of the University, was on 1 June 2002 admitted to the degree of DOCTOR OF PHILOSOPHY.*

Very slowly, he took apart the frame and ran his fingers over the certificate—over the historic seal, the name, the title—with a look of regret. He stared for a while at the left wall. He took a deep breath, put the certificate into a folder, and put the folder in the book.

The resulting melancholy of the room was broken by an inordinately chipper voice. "Did you remember to check that the bills were 1969*A*? You try to pass on knockoffs to people like this, and…Well, actually, I'd love to see that. Don't check."

Dr. O'Neill nearly knocked over his chair as he scrambled up. "But … *how?*"

The boyish figure standing there, shaking out a shaggy mane of tawny hair, smiled too big. "The daisy chains are a nice touch, but you need some along the floorboards. You've got a mouse-hole behind the mini-fridge. So, what about my retainer?"

Having regained his composure—pointedly so—Dr. O'Neill strode over and opened said mini-fridge. He removed a tall, frosty glass of milk and handed it over. Then he ventured, "Not to inquire too much, Rob, but isn't a glass of milk for a retainer in keeping with brownie protocols?"

"Them, certain dime-novel detectives, mice who also want cookies, ultraviolent dystopian thugs—don't even try to label me, Doc. I can go from milk to a nice Chianti in nothing flat."

"Noted." Dr. O'Neill, attempting to be ever so casual, also checked the bag of $20 bills once more, to make sure the year was right.

"Of course it is. So how's the master plan going?"

"Well enough. I'll let you know when I need you. The first part's just going to be coordination, finding the nexus point, making the initial deals, setting out, and…" He trailed off, before trying to smoothly trail into another sentence entirely. "And it doesn't trouble you?" He picked something off a far corner of his desk. "What I've done? What I may do?"

"That's just it, oh Captain, my Captain, or …" Rob took a look at the left wall of the room, then gave him a mocking bow. "…whatever it will be. What you're doing will trouble everyone. And that's more fun." He smiled, again too big. "Why do you ask, Doc? Do you think I'm scared of what you chipped off of old gates?" He stepped closer than any concept of personal space — and closer than someone fidgeting with slivers of wrought iron might expect. "Do you think I'll stab you in the back?"

"Rob, buddy," Dr. O'Neill spread his arms as much as possible while being careful with what he was holding. "No need to worry at all." He met the yellow eyes evenly. "I *know* you're going to stab me in the back. Just not yet."

Rob stepped back, still smiling. "That's why you're the smart guy. Remember, though, you're calling in a solid, not a guided tour. I'll be a distraction when you need it, but I'm not going to hold your hand. Making sure people *don't* get lost isn't any of my schticks."

Dr. O'Neill nodded. "Provided I get all the information I need, triangulating the locations should not be a problem," he said as he looked to examine the tiny scraps of wing-membrane pinned to the butterfly board.

Street Fair **is expected to be released in 2016**

Acknowledgements

We'd like to thank our spouses, Cody Armond and Jennifer Wolf, for their support, as well as our families: Bill, Carmen, Sam, Maggie, Ben, Jeanne, and Kiera Perkins, Gerry Cook, Carol Wells-Reed, Kelly and Scott Hendrix, and Matthew Lewis, who counts.

Thanks particularly to Matt and his fellow intense beta reader, Creel Gallagher Java, for their careful attention and invaluable feedback.

Thanks to artist Christopher Kovacs for the title page logo and to A.J. Downey for her assistance and perspective.

Thanks to the unnameable amount of friends and neighbors for sticking by us to this point. Thanks to those, particularly Crawford Comeaux, who provided resources on ADHD.

Thanks to all those who took the time to review any of our published works so far, with particular thanks to Amanda Hopkins for her swiftness and enthusiasm. Thanks to the New Authors community and the Writerpunk community for all the rallying. Thanks as ever to the AFK Elixirs and Eatery in Renton, Washington, for being such a great venue for book events.

And thanks to everyone who bothered to read this far.

We hope you'll join us again in each of the Four Lost Cities, which are a story admittedly much older than ours.

www.authorjeffreycook.com
www.punkwriters.com

About the Authors

Jeffrey Cook lives in Maple Valley, Washington, with his wife and three large dogs. He was born in Boulder, Colorado, but has lived all over the United States. He's the author of the *Dawn of Steam* trilogy of alternate-history/emergent Steampunk epistolary novels and of the YA Sci-fi thriller *Mina Cortez: From Bouquets to Bullets*. He's a founding contributing author of Writerpunk Press and has also contributed to a number of role-playing game books for Deep7 Press out of Seattle. When not reading, researching, or writing, Jeffrey enjoys role-playing games and watching football.

Katherine Perkins lives in Coralville, Iowa, with her husband and one extremely skittish cat. She was born in Lafayette, Louisiana, and will defend its cuisine on any field of honor. She is the editor of the *Dawn of Steam* series and serves as Jeff's co-author of various short stories, including those for the charity anthologies of Writerpunk Press. When not reading, researching, writing, or editing, she tries to remember what she was supposed to be doing.

Made in the USA
San Bernardino, CA
31 March 2018